"I'll nee ~~D0342885~~ **o both your b** **e on a continuous basis."**

Daria's eyes widened, reflecting curiosity and a startled wariness. "Excuse me?"

"If the Shey Group takes you on as a client, I'll be with you 24/7. You said you were hiring an accountant. That could be me."

She frowned, her eyebrows drawing downward. "But I wouldn't give my accountant the right to stay in my home. You did say twenty-four hours a day?"

Ryker grinned at her, suddenly pleased with his idea. Spending days and nights with this woman had an intimate appeal that intrigued him. All his life he'd been the boy from the bad part of town who had kept his distance, respected that certain lines were never crossed, but now he'd get to step across the line and see firsthand how the other half lived.

"You're going to take a romantic interest in your new accounatant."

Dear Harlequin Intrigue Reader,

Spring is in the air...and so is mystery. And just as always, Harlequin Intrigue has a spectacular lineup of breathtaking romantic suspense for you to enjoy.

Continuing her oh-so-sexy HEROES INC. trilogy, Susan Kearney brings us *Defending the Heiress*—which should say it all. As if anyone *wouldn't* want to be personally protected by a hunk!

Veteran Harlequin Intrigue author Caroline Burnes has crafted a super Southern gothic miniseries. THE LEGEND OF BLACKTHORN has everything—skeletons in the closet, a cast of unique characters and even a handsome masked phantom who rides a black stallion. And can he kiss! *Rider in the Mist* is the first of two classic tales.

The Cradle Mission by Rita Herron is another installment in her NIGHTHAWK ISLAND series. This time a cop has to protect his dead brother's baby and the beautiful woman left to care for the child. But why is someone dead set on rocking the cradle...?

Finally, Sylvie Kurtz leads us down into one woman's horror—so deep, she's all but unreachable...until she meets and trusts one man to lead her out of the darkness in *Under Lock and Key*.

We hope you savor all four titles and return again next month for more exciting stories.

Sincerely,

Denise O'Sullivan
Senior Editor
Harlequin Intrigue

DEFENDING
THE HEIRESS
SUSAN KEARNEY

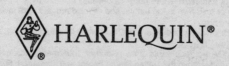

HARLEQUIN®

TORONTO • NEW YORK • LONDON
AMSTERDAM • PARIS • SYDNEY • HAMBURG
STOCKHOLM • ATHENS • TOKYO • MILAN • MADRID
PRAGUE • WARSAW • BUDAPEST • AUCKLAND

For Patricia Smith, an editor whose wise guidance
is much appreciated. Thanks, Patricia!

ISBN 0-373-22709-4

DEFENDING THE HEIRESS

Copyright © 2003 by Susan Hope Kearney

ABOUT THE AUTHOR

Susan Kearney used to set herself on fire four times a day. Now she does something really hot—she writes romantic suspense. While she no longer performs her signature fire dive (she's taken up figure skating), she never runs out of ideas for characters and plots. A business graduate from the University of Michigan, Susan is working on her next novel and writes full-time. She resides in a small town outside Tampa, Florida, with her husband and children and a spoiled Boston terrier. Visit her at http://www.SusanKearney.com.

Books by Susan Kearney

HARLEQUIN INTRIGUE

*The Sutton Babies
†Hide and Seek
**The Crown Affair
††Heroes, Inc.

CLASSIFIED

For Your Information.
Read and Destroy:

The SHEY GROUP is a private paramilitary organization whose purpose is to take on high-risk, high-stakes missions in accord with U.S. government policy. All members are former CIA, FBI or military with top-level clearances and specialized skills. Members maintain close ties to the intelligence community and conduct high-level behind-the-scenes operations for the government as well as for private individuals and corporations.

The U.S. government will deny any connection with this group.

Employ at your own risk.

CAST OF CHARACTERS

Daria Harrington—The heiress and CEO of a successful floral boutique business stands accused of murder. Desperate to prove her innocence, she hires a member of the mysterious Shey Group.

Ryker Stevens—Ex-Special Forces soldier with an MBA, Ryker has been assigned by the Shey Group's legendary founder, Logan Kincaid, to protect Daria and find out who is trying to destroy her.

Rudy Harrington—Daria's father, a business tycoon who thinks women should be wives and mothers. He's determined to turn over his empire to his only son.

Shandra Harrington—Daria's frivolous stepmother. Her main goal in life is to please her husband. But is she as harmless as she appears?

Peter Harrington—Daria's brother, the heir apparent to the Harrington empire. He doesn't intend to let anything stand in his way.

Elizabeth Hinze—Daria's friend and manager of the Fifth Avenue store. She's keeping a deadly secret.

Mike Brannigan—Daria's wealthy ex-boyfriend. He's been trying to buy her out for months and is getting more and more desperate. How far will he go to get what he wants?

Dear Reader,

Defending the Heiress is the second book in my HEROES, INC. miniseries. After stranding my characters in *Daddy to the Rescue* (HI #705) in the mountains, I was ready to move to the city. So this story takes place in the heart of Manhattan.

Daria Harrington is my kind of heroine, successful and intelligent and in trouble up to her beautiful neck. I matched her with Ryker Stevens, a man from the rough side of the tracks who now works for the Shey Group. His business savvy and computer skills may save Daria from jail, and he may eventually find the villain, but he's never before come up against a woman like Daria.

I hope you enjoy my efforts. I always look forward to hearing from readers, so please feel free to stop by my Web site and visit: www.SusanKearney.com. Best wishes!

Susan Kearney

Chapter One

"We need to slow down, delay the expansion," Daria Harrington told her twin sister Fallon with a touch of impatience.

Neither the full blush of white amaryllis in a striking cachepot on Daria's desk, nor the blooms' soothing fragrance, calmed her. The peaceful Warden serigraph depicting a cottage with warm lighted windows that her sister had recently purchased for her didn't ease Daria's agitation either.

"The meeting in Tokyo is set for next week," Fallon argued.

"Cancel it."

"Why?"

Daria forced her gaze from her slice of the New York skyline outside her office window to her sister, sitting in a guest chair beside her husband, Harry. "Growing our business with skyrocketing speed hasn't allowed enough time to build a proper foundation."

While Daria enjoyed staying in the city, putting down roots and tending the business, her more reckless vagabond sister preferred new adventures while traipsing around the world. Together they'd made a great team, opening their signature floral boutiques and expanding at a record pace. The partnership they'd started just out of college had succeeded beyond either of their most imaginative dreams.

But this time Daria would insist on delaying the new expansion into the Asian markets until they dealt with some pressing business issues here at home. She thrummed her fingers on the antique desk she'd purchased during college. Even back then she'd known she wanted a home with beautiful objects, and she'd started collecting on a meager budget. Now she no longer had to let price determine whether or not she could acquire Tarkay's newest painting or an antique emerald ring, but she no longer had the time to shop—for groceries, much less estate sales.

"Must I remind you that you wanted to delay opening Harrington Bouquet's London branch?" Fallon challenged her. "And London is now one of our best success stories."

Fallon swiped a lock of hair behind her ear, exchanged glances with her silent husband, Harry Levine, who simply shrugged. Daria thought Harry the perfect brother-in-law. Fully supportive of her sister and confident in his own abilities, he never interfered in the business. So far as she knew, he hadn't even muttered one protest after the wedding when Fallon had insisted on keeping her maiden name, Harrington. Intelligent and always alert, Harry spoke at least a dozen languages and enjoyed accompanying her sister in her gypsy lifestyle.

The problem wasn't Harry, but Fallon. Her sister wouldn't sit still and listen. Fallon never stayed in one place long enough to comprehend a problem, never mind help solve the underlying difficulties.

Fallon smiled at Daria. "We must grow with the market or risk becoming stagnant. With low interest rates and the worldwide economy strong, the time is ripe for expansion."

Fallon could talk the talk, but Daria didn't buy into the innocent smile or her sister's theory, no matter what spin she put on it. Daria simply had to find the words to convince her stubborn twin, who—already restless—stood and paced, making an elegant picture from the top of her neatly coiffed off-the-shoulder chestnut hair to her Dolce and Gabana dress and custom-made Italian pumps.

Daria tried again. "We have a lot to lose, Fallon. We aren't kids anymore. Due to Grandma Harrington's trust fund, and our ingenuity, we're successful."

"Thanks to our recent expansions in London, Paris, Milan and Sydney. What's wrong with opening more stores?"

"Because while you're off gallivanting around the world, I'm stuck in the New York office dealing with suppliers, shipping and legalese."

"Stuck?" Fallon spun and placed her hands on her hips. "You're stuck because you refuse to leave. How many times have I invited you overseas, but you always make up excuses to stay in that stifling penthouse you call home."

Daria wouldn't let her sister sidetrack her with her critique of the fashionable penthouse Daria had turned into her personal haven. Despite Fallon's propensity for fine clothing and makeup, she didn't care if she lived out of the back of a bus. Daria appreciated her creature comforts, which included clean sheets, a hot soak in her tub and her cats.

"My running the corporation wasn't our deal, remember? You were going to share the paperwork—"

"But you're so good at it." Fallon tried flattery, but Daria simply raised an eyebrow that needed shaping since she'd had to cancel her last three waxing appointments in order to deal with pressing business.

"I'm good at the paperwork because I *do* it."

"And I'm good at opening stores. Let me do my job."

"That's what I'm telling you." Daria released an exasperated sigh. "Right now your job needs to be here in New York. With me. The paperwork is too much for one person."

"You need a man in your life to distract you."

"That might be nice," Daria replied. "I don't have time to go out on dates. I don't leave here until after eleven and fall asleep exhausted, then get up at five and start all over again. And why am I working so hard? Because you keep opening new stores and creating more paperwork. It's time to assess our company, enjoy life a little."

"I'm enjoying life," Fallon answered.

"But I'm working too hard. I can barely find time for the Big Sister program. I want a change."

Fallon stared at her, no doubt assessing Daria's determination. Unlike her sister, Daria didn't enjoy conflict, but she wasn't giving in—not this time.

Daria liked life to run smoothly, so usually she let Fallon have her way. But not this time. No matter how much her stomach clenched into a hard knot from having to deal with the conflict, she would win.

As children, the sisters had reacted differently to

their wealthy but cold and demanding father, who had remarried shortly after their parents' divorce. They had lived with their mother for one year until her death, then returned to live with their father and his new wife.

Shuffled from nanny to boarding school to summer camps, the only consistency in their lives was one another. While the two sisters couldn't have been closer, they were very different people. Fallon avoided facing the lack of parental love and support in their lives by constantly changing her locales and friends. Daria reacted differently, building a comfy spot for herself wherever she happened to be.

And Daria depended on her sister's honest opinions, her friendship and her love. Since they'd been kids, they'd always backed one another, stood up for one another. Daria could count the arguments they'd had on one hand.

"You want to sell the business? Retire?" Fallon asked in astonishment.

"I was thinking about a vacation and, afterward, I want to work only three or four days a week." Then she could spend a full day with Tanya, a kid in the Big Sister program where she volunteered her free time—when she had free time. "But I can't leave the office when my partner isn't here to take over when I'm gone."

"But—"

"Look. I know you won't be happy until you've built a Harrington Bouquet in every major city of the world. But we need to hire more people, delegate."

Daria was sure her sister understood the points she was making, but Fallon often refused to use her inborn intelligence out of sheer stubbornness. The boring business details didn't excite her sister as much as traveling to a foreign city, finding the perfect location and then creating a shop in the image of their original New York office boutique.

If Fallon had had her way, she would have made each shop different and unique, but Daria had insisted they look exactly the same for cohesiveness. That was one battle she'd won. Each Harrington Bouquet possessed the same unique layout, the same Berber carpeting and mahogany showcases, the same exquisite quality of customer service. Each sold exotic floral arrangements shipped from greenhouses in North and South America, East Africa and the Far East. The stores' clients came from the powerful and wealthy, the world's elite. Rock stars, actresses, opera divas, royalty, owners of Fortune 500 companies—all of these clients relied on Harrington Bouquets to liven up special occasions, including anniversaries, promotions, birthdays, opening nights, weddings and funerals.

Stalling for time, Daria rose to her feet. "How about fresh coffee?"

She didn't wait for her sister's answer, simply ambled to the antique sideboard, which was protected by delicate Irish-lace doilies. While Daria never drank coffee, much preferring green tea, she always kept her sister's favorite Jamaican Blue Mountain roast perking for their infrequent meetings. Daria opened a tin of lemon-raspberry shortbread, chocolate buttons and pecan chews. After placing steaming mugs on a silver tray beside the cookies, she poured herself a cup of tea. "Here you go."

"Thank you." Fallon's eyes lit up at the sight of the pecan chews. "If you're thinking to bribe me—"

Daria rolled her eyes in exasperation. "Nothing is further from my mind."

Tall, dark and with a scar on his handsome chin, Harry chuckled, then helped himself to a chocolate button, which he happily dipped into his coffee and then popped into his mouth. He crunched away, dipping one cookie after another, not the least bit concerned by the calories.

Fallon lifted her coffee cup into the air and saluted Daria as if to take the sting from her words. "I've already committed to looking at a site in Tokyo." She downed a quarter cup of coffee in one giant gulp.

"Cancel anyway." Daria resisted the cookies and sipped her tea. Unlike her svelte sister and Harry, she needed to watch her weight. Fallon was tall and slender while Daria was short and curvy. They shared two features in common, their light chestnut hair and their hazel eyes, but Daria had inherited the petiteness of her mother's family while Fallon had the long, lanky genes of the Harringtons, who stayed thin, no doubt due to their restless metabolisms. Unfortunately, whatever Daria put in her mouth seemed to go directly to her thighs.

So while Fallon sipped and ate, Daria spoke. "At least stay long enough to help me hire an in-house accountant and another purchasing agent and floral designer to take off some of the load."

"I suppose I could do that." Fallon yawned and covered her mouth. "Sorry. I'm more tired than I'd thought. I'm needing this caffeine buzz just to keep my eyes open." She guzzled more coffee.

Daria realized that as usual the two sisters had found a way to compromise, but while she had Fallon in the office, she intended to bounce her other ideas off her sister. "We also might want to think about purchasing another greenhouse. An accountant could run the numbers and help make an informed decision. Isabelle could use help in the purchasing department, and Cindy is overwhelmed doubling as designer and consumer specialist. Our volume is almost…"

Daria glanced at Harry. The shock had her stopping in midsentence. Harry had fallen asleep!

Quiet but oh-so-alert Harry who never missed a detail and could party all night and never so much as yawned the following day had closed his eyes right in the middle of the morning. His chin plummeted onto his chest with a thud.

Fallon must have been just as surprised as Daria because she suddenly dropped her cup. But she made no move to avoid the hot coffee spilling on her designer dress.

Daria's horrified gaze shot from Harry to her sister. Fallon's yawn had disappeared and was replaced by an unnatural paralysis.

"Fallon? What's wrong?"

Fallon didn't answer. Within seconds, her sister's eyes dilated, her pupils enlarging so much that Daria could barely see the whites of Fallon's eyes. Her face masklike, her expression fixed straight ahead as if she'd been drugged, Fallon didn't move. Didn't scream.

Harry's face had the same deathlike mask as her sister's.

Daria didn't waste one second checking for a pulse. Scrambling to the phone, tripping once, she dialed 911. "I need an ambulance."

The operator, her voice calm in contrast to Daria's

spiking fear, confirmed her address and asked the nature of the emergency.

"They aren't moving. Or breathing. Hurry."

"They?"

"My sister and her husband." Harry's chest wasn't going up and down. Her sister stared sightless at the ceiling. "Oh, God. I think they're dead."

"Is there a pulse?"

On knees weak with terror, Daria knelt and felt her sister's neck, then Harry's. She might have missed the pulse, but she knew with an icy dread and horror that even if the paramedics materialized inside her office right now, they wouldn't be able to revive them.

Six weeks later

RYKER STEVENS BLINKED as a knock interrupted his latest attempt to integrate an unbreakable encryption program with his operating system. The techies down at Langley had come up with an awesome Java script, but installing the bugger had him bummed after he'd crashed his computer for the third time. Now nothing worked.

The door of his office opened. As Ryker took in his visitor, he lost all interest in his computer for the first time in several weeks. How could he think about software with the achy-breaky-heart hardware coming in his direction?

A high-maintenance woman like this one had never graced Ryker Stevens's office before, and he could barely hold back an appreciative whistle. She didn't just walk, she strode toward him with a sexy sway of hips encased in a flowing black ankle-length skirt that ended at leather boots. Her soft tailored blouse welled and nipped in at just the right places. He raised his eyes to her face, and she attempted a tentative smile of greeting, which failed.

This woman didn't need to smile to look good. She didn't need the designer clothes she wore to draw attention to her killer body or the expertly applied makeup to improve her skin. Lordy, she was perfect, hot, except for the dark circles under her eyes that her makeup couldn't quite hide. She was the kind of woman a man fantasized about after he fell asleep surfing the Net, then woke up to find it'd all been a dream. Women like her came from uptown, the other side of the tracks, and they rarely sized him up with burdened hazel eyes that told him trouble weighed on her like a five-hundred-pound monster.

"Are you Ryker Stevens?" She spoke in a voice rough and low as if she'd spent too many hours in long conversations or smoke-filled rooms.

"That depends on who wants to know." Ryker had been in tough spots quite a few times in his thirty years, and he immediately recognized the combination of hope and desperation on her expressive face.

"Let's not play games." The stranger opened her purse, took out a gold pen and a checkbook in elegant gilded leather. She scrawled her name across the signature spot, ripped a blank check free and shoved it across his desk, leaving him to fill in his name and the dollar amount. He wondered if the lady was usually into grand gestures, because she didn't seem the type. Despite her display of boldness, she was classy, refined, understated.

He read the name printed across the top of the check—Daria Harrington—then ignored the payment, making no move to touch the check. But suddenly Ryker's prodigious memory and ability to sort through seemingly stray facts kicked in. An old acquaintance of his, Harry Levine, had married a Harrington. If this woman was Harry's wife, his old friend had not only married money and class but beauty, too. Harry had invited him to the wedding, but he'd received the invitation months too late after returning from a mission in Saudi Arabia. Some guys had all the luck—even if their wives didn't take their names after the wedding ceremony.

"You're Harry Levine's wife?"

"Sister-in-law," she corrected him, and before he could decide how he felt about that news, she threw him a zinger. "Harry's dead. I killed him."

Ryker would have laughed at the impossibility of that statement, except, at the admission, her back straightened and her face paled. She tipped her chin up, but her lower lip quivered.

"Was it an accident?" he asked.

"I murdered him."

She couldn't have shocked him more if she'd claimed to be an alien from Mars.

Harry Levine, one of the CIA's top operatives, dead? Killed by *her* after some of the most highly trained and skilled agents in the world had tried and failed?

Ryker cursed himself for holing up in his office to

work steadily since he'd returned from Zaire, instead of paying attention to the news. He'd been living on pizza and Chinese food for weeks. Since his office was the front room of his apartment, he could delve into a problem for as long as he wanted without leaving his place. Running a hand through his ragged hair, he tried to recall exactly how long it had been since he'd read a newspaper, watched television, called up a headline on the Internet or even listened to a radio. Maybe several weeks. No wonder he hadn't heard about Harry's death, which had to have made the papers since he'd married into such a prominent family.

He stared at Daria. From her chin-length chestnut hair down to her expensive boots, she looked like a socialite, a debutante, as if she belonged in the pages of a fashion magazine. Her eyes held his, but he sensed the effort it took. He saw determination, but not the eyes of a killer. Besides, wealthy daughters of prominent citizens usually didn't commit murder and then openly admit it. Yet Daria Harrington would hardly have come here claiming to be a murderer if she didn't believe her statement. Unless she was crazy.

She didn't look crazy. She looked worried.

And her brother-in-law had pulled Ryker's ass out of the fire once in Beijing and again in Panama. If not for Harry's impeccable timing and bravery, Ryker might still be rotting in a foreign prison. So he owed Harry, and even if Ryker did come from poor white trash, he always paid his debts.

That he had minutes ago been fantasizing over Harry's murderer disgusted him. And angered him.

His voice was colder than he'd intended. "Please have a seat, Ms. Harrington."

"Where?" She looked at the only other chair in the room. It was filled with old circuit boards, a mouse, a broken motherboard, an Ethernet card and several empty pizza boxes.

He leaned over his desk, tilted the chair, ignored the crash as the equipment and trash toppled onto the floor, then righted the chair. He supposed he should have stood and offered her a seat right off, maybe a drink to put her at ease. But what did he care about putting Harry's murderer at ease?

He still didn't completely believe she'd killed Harry, and he intended to get the entire story from her—especially why she wanted to hire him. If what she said was true, if she'd killed Harry, he was the last person to come to for help.

Had her rich father with his connections galore suggested she hire the services of the Shey Group? But money wasn't enough to hire the team Ryker worked with. They only accepted the cases of the good guys. The Shey Group wasn't just pricey, they were picky.

As a covert team of men with top-secret government clearances, the Shey Group took on dangerous and seemingly impossible missions. They had the luxury of turning down more assignments than they accepted, despite the very hefty fees they charged.

Ryker loved the interesting nature of his work. Top-secret clearances meant access to the latest technological wizardry. And their boss Logan Kincaid's unique and close ties to the intelligence community, as well as his influence, which was rumored to reach directly into the White House, allowed the team access to information unavailable to private citizens.

Even if Daria convinced Ryker to help her, he'd have to take the mission to Logan Kincaid for approval. Although the team worked together, they were a loose-knit organization, living in different parts of the country between missions. Kincaid believed in paying his people well, in allowing them partial ownership in the Shey Group, and he preferred the team to rest well between their often dangerous missions. Ryker wondered what Kincaid would think about what Daria was about to tell him.

At a time like this, his sophisticated leader would no doubt fall back on impeccable manners and the most courteous of tones, giving himself time to fully assess the situation. But the polite manners of society hadn't been drilled into Ryker early enough to come automatically. As a child he'd been too busy dodging the slaps of his alcoholic father. In college he'd worked three jobs to pay his way through.

The kind of women who didn't need to say a word for others to recognize that they shopped in the upscale department stores and breezed through life on daddy's connections usually had no interest in Ryker, nor he in them, so he hadn't had much practice dealing with a lady like Daria Harrington.

Nope, Ms. Daria Harrington certainly wasn't his usual type, but she fascinated him as she tried to withhold her dismay at his messy office. Especially as dust from the spilled materials rose up from the floor and caused her to sneeze.

"Sorry."

She took several tissues out of her purse and used one to wipe her almost-perfect nose all so delicately. With a second tissue, she wiped the dust from his chair before sitting on the edge with her back ramrod stiff. She acted as though slouching or relaxing was a shooting offense.

And for the life of him, he couldn't understand how the woman could worry about dust on her chair after the bombshell she'd just dropped on him. But people reacted differently to stress.

"How did you find me?" he asked.

"Harry's attorney told me to hire you."

The Shey Group had hired Harry's attorney when they'd needed legal counsel. So it wasn't surprising that she'd shown up here.

"Why don't you start at the beginning?" he suggested, working to keep his tone civil.

She replied almost primly. "Six weeks ago, Harry and Fallon, my sister, came to my office for a meeting."

"About?"

"It doesn't matter."

"Let me be the judge of that." At her startled jerk he added, "Okay?" to soften his statement. He had to remind himself that this woman had probably never been questioned roughly. But he was getting ahead of himself.

"Fallon came to my office at my request. Harry always accompanies her, but never interferes, never interfered, in the business." She'd corrected her tense as if she had trouble remembering or believing that

Harry was actually dead. "My sister wanted to open a branch in Tokyo and—"

"What kind of work do you do?" he asked, finding himself more intrigued by the minute. He'd figured her for one of those women who did charity work and spent the rest of the day having her nails done. So much for first impressions. But then he'd always been better with machines than people.

"We own, I own, Harrington Bouquet."

"The fancy flower shops?" He should have realized sooner. But first she'd bowled him over with her looks and then swept him away by her murder confession.

She nodded. "Fallon was opening new shops faster than I could keep up with the paperwork."

He couldn't imagine this woman hunching over a desk dealing with paperwork, and realized he'd judged her more like a kid from the poor side of the tracks than a man who had seen more than his share of the world. Lots of wealthy women worked. He knew that, once he actually stopped to think. And he recalled from a business article in the *Wall Street Journal*, which he'd read last year during a trip from Casablanca to Istanbul, that Harrington Bouquet was quite the success story.

"You and your sister argued?"

"We disagreed at first, but had come to a compromise. She agreed to stay in New York long enough to help me hire more in-house staff."

"And Harry took no part in this discussion?"

"I don't believe he said a word."

"Okay. What happened next?"

She didn't shift uncomfortably in her chair. If anything, she held every muscle tight, holding perfectly still. "I served them coffee and opened a tin of cookies. They drank the coffee, ate the cookies and then… they died."

"How?"

"From the way they looked as they died and the questions the police asked me, I'm fairly certain they were poisoned. The police probably think I poisoned either the cookies or the coffee."

"Why aren't you in jail?"

"The only reason I haven't been arrested is that the toxicology reports aren't back yet. That and the fact that I passed a polygraph test."

"I see."

Her explanation certainly illuminated how she might have fooled Harry. The CIA operative wouldn't have expected his sister-in-law to poison him. If she'd attempted to employ a weapon, she wouldn't have stood a chance. But spiking coffee or cookies with poison—a woman's trick—had taken Ryker's old acquaintance by surprise. And if she was that underhanded, she might know how to fool the lie detector, since the machines were only as good as their operators.

As if realizing what Ryker needed to know without him prodding her further, probably from her statements to the police, she added, "I never drink coffee, and I didn't eat any of the cookies since I have to watch my weight." Her voice dropped. "But I didn't… at least not…on purpose. I didn't *know* about the poison. I loved my sister, and I loved my brother-in-law. I would never do anything to deliberately hurt them. You must believe me.'' She dropped her face into her hands. "Oh, God. I promised myself I wouldn't beg, but I don't believe the police will ever clear my name. And even more important, my sister and Harry's killer is out there somewhere, free to murder someone else. I want justice for them.''

Chapter Two

Daria raised her head and spoke in a flat tone. "I don't believe the police are even considering another suspect."

"Why?" Ryker asked again.

"They took my computer, they're questioning my employees and my friends. The investigation seems focused on me. Me and only me. What unnerves me is that they're so positive I'm guilty they aren't even looking at any other possibilities. If they continue as they are, Fallon and Harry will never have justice."

"And what exactly do you want from me?" Ryker asked, considering whether or not to speak to his boss about taking her case. And he wasn't sure why. Maybe he admired the strength he saw in her as she so valiantly tried to hold back tears. He certainly respected the intelligent way she'd laid out the facts and the courage she'd exhibited by coming here alone. He wondered why her family hadn't accompanied her and whether they blamed her for her sister's murder.

She leaned forward slightly in the chair. "I want you to find Harry and Fallon's real killer. Will you do it?" She glanced from the blank check on the desk back to his face.

"I'll need much more information first. And my boss will have to approve this mission."

She straightened up, all signs of her tears gone. "Harry's lawyer told me Logan Kincaid's a fine man. And he liked you, too. That's why I came here."

He ignored the soft plea in her tone. He didn't mention that if she turned out to be guilty, justice for Harry might mean her spending her life behind bars.

Without leaving his office, Ryker could start an investigation. His specialty was computer research, and his first rule of inquiry was to find, analyze and follow the money trail. Yet, he also knew that investigating motivations for criminal actions often produced good results, too. "You and Fallon are the sole owners of this business?"

"Yes."

"And with Fallon and Harry now out of the picture…?"

"I own it all." She held her head high. "That's why I'm the prime suspect. According to the police, I had means, opportunity and motive."

"I understand their logic."

"But I have no need for more money," she protested.

Yeah, right. "I see."

He'd answered noncommittally, totally unwilling to believe her statement. Not for the first time he wondered if she was lying to him, putting her own spin on the truth. Who didn't need more money except maybe Bill Gates?

Her hands shook and she took one into the other to control the trembling. "I was framed. But the worst part, the absolute worst part, is knowing *I* gave Harry and Fallon that poison."

Despite the rigidity of her body, she shuddered slightly, and even through his skepticism he couldn't help sympathizing with what she was going through. Obviously she found the memory of her sister's and Harry's deaths extremely painful. But was she feeling remorse and regret?

Ryker had the urge to go to her and comfort her but he didn't. However, he couldn't let her rip herself up without trying to console her, either. Not after he'd heard the raw pain in her voice that she'd tried and failed to hide. If he couldn't hold her, he could at least attempt to give words of comfort.

He didn't have to force genuine warmth or concern into his voice. "If you didn't know what was in the coffee or cookies, you can't blame yourself."

As she remembered the deaths, he had to steel himself against the bleakness in her eyes. "Poison is not a good way to die."

The childhood memory of a policeman pulling back his own mother's bloody face from a smashed windshield after a traffic accident that had killed her flashed through his mind. The blood on the cracked glass still gave him occasional nightmares. "There's no good way to die."

"I always wanted to go in my sleep," she admitted somewhat timidly, yet her eyes flashed with a certain defiance, too, daring fate, apparently, to see what her future held.

"If you die in your sleep, then you don't get to say goodbye."

His statement seemed to startle her for a moment, as if she wanted to ask him why he thought the way he did, but then she pulled back into herself.

"Will you help me?" she asked again.

Despite the plea in those appealing hazel eyes, Ryker didn't immediately answer Daria's question. In fact, he refused to meet her eyes. For the moment, he wanted to keep a clear head, and he refused to allow her grief to influence his decision.

He made up his mind by going with his gut feelings, then told her what he needed. "For starters, I'd like you to try and write down for me every question that the homicide detectives asked you. I also need a list of everyone who has access to your office, your purse and your home. Everyone. Cleaning people, employees, friends, family. Lovers?"

"No one right now."

"Ex-lovers, then." Ruthlessly he shut down any personal reaction to her admission that she was depending on him. "I'll also need a separate list of people who know that you don't drink coffee and that your sister did. Meanwhile, I'll try to obtain a copy of the police and autopsy reports."

"You can do that?"

"I have an old friend in the medical examiner's office and Logan Kincaid is…connected."

She took a pen and pad out of her purse and made several quick notes. "What else?"

"I'll need access to your office. And I'll need an inventory of every poisonous cleaning agent in your office."

"What about poisonous flowers and plants?"

"Those, too."

She handed him a business card, then removed a spare key from her key ring and placed it on top of the blank check. "I'll have most of the information you requested ready by tomorrow afternoon."

He made his next statement as matter-of-fact as the

others and watched her closely to gauge her reaction. "I'll also need to insert myself into both your business and your personal life on a continuous basis."

Her eyes widened, the hazel in them reflecting curiosity and a startled wariness. "Excuse me?"

"If the Shey Group takes you on as a client, I'll be with you 24/7. You said you were hiring an accountant. That could be me. While I don't have a CPA's license, I do have an MBA, and the job would give me the opportunity to go through the books, ask questions in every department."

She frowned, her eyebrows drawing downward. "But I wouldn't give my accountant the right to stay in my home. You did say twenty-four hours a day?"

He grinned at her, suddenly pleased with his idea. Spending days and nights with this woman had an intimate appeal that intrigued him. All his life he'd been the boy from the bad part of town who had kept his distance, respected that certain lines were never crossed, but now he'd get to step across the line and see firsthand how the other half lived.

He leaned back in his chair and laced his fingers behind his head. "You're going to take a romantic interest in your new accountant."

She shook her head. "Look, I'll do whatever it takes to find Fallon and Harry's killer. But no one will believe we've suddenly hooked up."

He rocked back even farther in his chair and lifted a brow. "Really?"

"I just lost my sister. I've been grieving. And even if I could fake grabbing on to you to ease my sorrow, I never mix business and pleasure."

"You'll make an exception."

"No one will believe that I'm starting an affair

with my new accountant when I'm being accused of murder.''

''Why not?''

''Because...'' She hesitated, searched for words, then threw her hands into the air. ''That's not me.''

''What do you mean?''

''I don't do affairs. I don't do one-night stands. And I don't do flings.''

''Never?''

''Never.''

''I suppose you don't go on casual dates?'' he challenged her.

''Sure, I date.'' The hazel in her eyes deepened to a steady green flame. ''But I don't *ever* bring a casual date back to my home. And my family and friends know how I feel. The only way to make a relationship between us believable is if I pretend to have fallen in love with you. And how likely is that while I'm facing a murder charge?''

''Of course people will believe you,'' he insisted. ''The enormous stress you're under can alter the behavioral patterns of a lifetime. You can't deal with the pressure alone, and so you turn to your handsome, brilliant—''

''—and oh-so-modest—''

''—new accountant to lean on.''

''I'm not in the habit of leaning on anyone—'' her voice broke ''—except Fallon.''

''But now you need me. All you have to do is be convincing and people will buy your act.''

''I'm a businesswoman not an actress. And what you're asking me to do will provoke the suspicions of my family and friends.''

She sounded so positive. He raised an eyebrow. "You sure you aren't overreacting?"

"Look, I've owned my penthouse apartment for two years. You'll be the first man I've ever invited inside."

Obviously she didn't think much of his plan. But he needed to be with her to help her. The lady's back was up against the wall. So he pushed and ended the meeting. "I don't see another way to go. I'll call my boss and get back to you tomorrow."

DARIA CHECKED her watch. Six o'clock. She should go back to her office. Between meetings with her attorney, interviews with the cops and avoiding the press, work had piled up.

But it was going on alone that weighed so heavily on her heart. The work that had once brought her so much joy seemed empty without Fallon. Harrington Bouquet had meant the world to both of them because they'd succeeded together. Yet if Fallon was still here, she would tell Daria to go on for both of them.

Daria forced her mind back to the business. She would have thought that since the bad publicity over Fallon's and Harry's deaths, business would be off. But the old saying that any publicity, even bad publicity, was good for business must be true. Harrington Bouquet could barely keep up with the orders.

And now she couldn't even hire an accountant to take off some of the load. Not with Ryker Stevens intent on claiming the position. Daria hoped she'd done the right thing by throwing herself on his mercy, but she felt she had to. She didn't think that even her high-priced attorney believed in her innocence. And if he didn't believe her, he would be looking for legal technicalities to get her off instead of finding justice for Fallon and Harry.

Someone like Ryker Stevens wouldn't be concerned with legal maneuvering. He had struck her as a man who aimed for his target and was accustomed to striking the bull's-eye. Direct, honest—he was just what she needed to boost her confidence and strength to keep fighting.

She couldn't cry anymore. She'd had to do something, and after speaking with Ryker her confidence that she might eventually find her sister and brother-in-law's murderer rose a smidgen.

With a sigh she slipped behind the wheel of her car and drove toward her office. While owning a car was totally impractical in the city, she loved driving. She didn't mind the traffic, including trucks or taxi drivers, and just merged with the flow.

All too soon she arrived at the garage where she leased parking space that cost a small fortune. Well lit and guarded, the garage was conveniently across the street from Harrington Bouquet Number One— their very first store. Apparently the reporters hanging around outside had finally gone home and she could get some work done. From her parking place Daria could see the manager, Elizabeth, closing the shop, the assistants placing the unsold arrangements in large refrigeration units where the flowers would stay fresh. The Open sign winked out, although the elegant lavender sign advertising the shop remained on.

Normally, Daria wouldn't have waited for everyone to leave before she entered the building, but she was simply too tired to put on a brave face. After fortifying herself with a cup of hot tea—tea that came directly from a sealed packet in case she, too, might be a target for the poisoner—she intended to go straight to her office and work, probably until midnight.

But the moment she unlocked the door that served as her private entrance, she sensed someone in the darkness.

She flipped on the light. "Ryker?"

What was he doing here?

Before she could ask him, she heard voices coming from her office. Ryker put a finger to his lips, signaling her to be silent. Then he cocked his head upstairs, a gesture that he wanted her to listen.

The familiar voices of her family drifted down to her. Damn. She didn't want to see or speak to them. Not to her powerful father, who had never once approved of anything she did, nor to her simpering stepmother, Shandra, who lived to please her husband, nor even her half brother, Peter, the pride of the family. Everyone liked Peter—even she and Fallon liked the young heir to the Harrington dynasty.

"Mom, we shouldn't be here," Peter insisted.

"Your father believes we need a family chat away from the servants," Shandra told him in her deep Boston accent. "Daria's been avoiding us. We are her family, and she didn't even come to the special church memorial after Fallon and Harry's funeral."

Daria had gone to the funeral, but she couldn't bear to put up a brave front any longer, so she'd gone home.

The disapproval in her father's tone was unmistakable, even as he defended her. "She sent flowers."

"For the sake of the family," Shandra complained, "we all need to keep up appearances. Even Daria."

"She's grieving in her own way," Peter argued.

"Fallon and Daria were close. Can you imagine how she feels?"

"Who cares how she feels?" Shandra asked. "What matters is what she does."

"What she's done is drag the Harrington name through the mud." Daddy's predictable roar of anger merely showed that he cared more about the Harrington name than he did about the death of his daughter. In her father's eyes, daughters were good for only one thing—marriage and giving him grandchildren, preferably grandsons. And both daughters had failed him. Daria because she'd remained single and Fallon because she'd married a "nobody."

Harry Levine hadn't been from old money or even from new money. That he'd been bright and witty and a loving husband didn't count—not to Rudolf Harrington.

As Daria listened to her family squabble, she wondered what had put Ryker on alert. He was tense, his muscles tight, almost as if he expected to fight off an attacker.

She hadn't expected to hear from him until tomorrow. So what was he doing here, arriving before she had and skulking around in the dark? Eavesdropping on her family's private conversation.

"I told you that we should have made an appointment," Shandra whined.

"I don't need a damn appointment to speak with my own daughter," her father fumed.

"You do if she won't take your phone calls." Peter sounded bored. "Not that I blame her after the way you acted at the funeral. A hug might have been appropriate."

"Peter, don't criticize your father. Harringtons don't show affection in public."

"She and Fallon were always tight. Daria had to have been hurting."

"She didn't shed one tear." Shandra's shrill tone sounded almost pleased.

"Mother, not everyone wears their emotions on their sleeve." Peter spoke to his parents without fear of reprisal. Always the favorite, he'd grown up spoiled, but he had the gumption to stand up to his parents, and Daria admired him for it. He'd stood next to her at the funeral and he was standing up for her again, now.

"Mom, if you'd stop protecting Dad, maybe he'd learn some manners."

"That's enough." Rudolf must have been desperate to talk to her if he'd come all the way across town. He'd never been in her office before. He probably bought flowers from her competitors. The thought smarted. No matter how predictable her father was, his coldness never quite stopped hurting her.

Beside her, Ryker placed a hand on her shoulder. "I spoke to Logan Kincaid on my cell phone as I drove here. He okayed the job." Before relief washed over her, he continued, "Why don't you introduce me to your family."

"You sure?"

He nodded. "Don't forget. I'm the new love of your life."

Her heart skittered a few beats before settling. "Daddy will have your background checked out within the hour."

"I'm good to go."

The Shey Group worked fast. Too fast. She wasn't

ready. To fake a relationship, she and Ryker should
have at least discussed the basics—like where and
how they'd supposedly met. But Daria took one look
at his determined face and saw a predatory gleam in
Ryker's eyes.

Her father might be about to meet his match.

"PLEASED TO MEET YOU, sir." Ryker offered to shake
hands with the distinguished silver-haired father of his
client. The head of the Harrington family rose to his
feet from behind the desk until the two men stood eye
to eye.

Rudolf shook hands and glanced from Ryker to
Daria and back. "You have me at a disadvantage,
sir."

Clearly, Harrington Sr. wanted an explanation for
Ryker's presence. Mrs. Harrington watched her husband for clues as to how to react, while Peter feigned
boredom. Interesting.

Deliberately, Ryker ignored Harrington Sr.'s comment. Instead, he turned what he hoped was an ador-
ing look on Daria. "I didn't expect to meet your family so soon."

Amusement sparkled in Daria's hazel eyes as she
strode over and slipped her arm through his. "I didn't
want to scare you off."

"Did she just insult us?" Mrs. Harrington asked,
her face smooth from Botox injections and unable to
frown.

Peter grinned. "Mother, don't start."

Rudolf glared at Daria. "What the hell have you
done now?"

"Why, Daddy." Ryker could have sworn from
Daria's lighthearted tone that she was enjoying her-

self. "I've done what you've always wanted. I've fallen in love."

Rudolf's face turned an angry shade of red. "Shandra, did my daughter just tell me that—"

"I'm afraid she did."

Her parents stared at Daria as if she'd just grown three heads. Even Peter's boredom had been replaced by wide-eyed astonishment. Obviously, Daria hadn't exaggerated when she'd explained that she was extremely choosy about her lovers.

Rudolf's fierce gaze narrowed on Ryker. "And just how long has this...this state of affairs been going on?"

"Sir, Daria's over twenty-one," Ryker said politely, softly, to take the sting out of his words.

"She's still my concern. Daria is my daughter," Rudolf protested.

"A grown-up daughter," Daria added defiantly. She straightened as if she'd donned invisible body armor that would protect her.

Ryker took Daria's hand, surprised to find her skin cold and clammy. "Is there a reason for your visit?"

Rudolf sank back into the chair behind the desk as if that position automatically gave him power. "We're here on family business, so if you would excuse us..."

"I don't think so." Ryker made himself comfortable, half sitting on the edge of her desk.

"Then why don't you tell us about yourself," Rudolf said.

"Look, I appreciate the fact that you're so eager to learn about me, but—" Ryker shot Daria a warm look "—we have work to do."

"Work?" Peter asked.

Daria placed a possessive hand on Ryker's shoulder. Although her words were businesslike, her implication was anything but. "I've hired Ryker to help me."

"In what capacity?" her father challenged.

"What do you care?" Daria shot right back. "You've never before taken an interest in Harrington Bouquet or my private life."

"You've never needed me before." Her father removed a cigar from his pocket. "I came to help."

Daria reached over the desk, took the cigar from her father's fingers and stuck it back in his pocket. "Don't light that. It's bad for the plants, never mind my lungs."

Peter flopped into a chair. "Daria, you better listen to him. He's trying to help in his own way."

Daria arched an eyebrow. "Really?"

Rudolf eyed Ryker then ignored him to focus on his daughter. "My sources inside the police department tell me that the toxicology report has come back. Your sister and Harry died from ingesting the nectar of Passion Perfect with their coffee."

"Passion Perfect?" Ryker asked.

Despite the dented armor, Daria stood straighter. "It's an exotic flower from the Brazilian rain forest. Harrington Bouquet is the only florist in North America that imports that particular flower."

"There's more." Her father placed the unlit cigar between his teeth.

Peter threw his hands into the air in disgust. "Oh, for God's sake. Tell her, Dad."

"It appears that you left e-mail correspondence on your computer."

"So?"

"In those e-mails, you discuss Passion Perfect's toxicity levels with your supplier."

"No, I didn't," she denied with a touch of surprise and annoyance. "I discussed price, quantity and shipments—never toxicity levels. They must be mistaken."

"The police were going to charge you with premeditated murder."

"What do you mean, they *were?*"

"Apparently, there's a technical problem. Your computer has a virus that could have allowed someone to alter your e-mail. I don't understand the details."

Ryker did. Hackers could get into any computer connected to the Internet, and if an unwary user opened an attachment, any files, including e-mails, could be modified by the hacker. Since her computer had a virus, the police couldn't know for sure whether Daria had written the incriminating e-mails or if someone had tried to frame her.

If Ryker could get his hands on her computer, he might be able to trace the hack back to the source. On his own, he couldn't swing that kind of cooperation with the cops, but Logan Kincaid could.

Daria looked pleased. "That's good news, then. Maybe the police will now believe that someone framed me."

"I'm afraid it's not that simple," her father sighed. "Your computer disappeared from the police evidence room last night."

So much for tracing the hacker through her system—but Ryker knew other ways. So would the hacker.

"First someone frames me and then they steal the

evidence that would lead back to them?'' Daria looked both thoughtful and angry.

''As a personal favor to me, the chief of police is looking into it. And the mayor has leaned on the district attorney to delay your arrest while these improprieties are being investigated.''

''I have the office's tape backups at home.'' Daria's voice rose with hope. ''Maybe I should invite the police over to investigate.''

That she wanted to protect the chain of evidence showed him that Daria could think on her feet, even under attack from her family. What she didn't know was that the police probably wouldn't accept the taped backups as evidence since she'd had time to alter them to show anything she wished.

''And maybe you shouldn't go to the police,'' Peter argued. ''They might *lose* the evidence again.''

Daria nodded. ''You've got a point.''

''Why don't you let me handle this?'' Her father took a passport out of his pocket and placed it on the desk. ''Leave the country while you still can.''

Daria trembled but made no move to take the passport. ''The police gave you the passport they took from me?''

''It's a new one. Use it.''

So the old man wanted his daughter out of the picture, and he'd gone to some trouble to see her on her way. Fake passports weren't easy to come by, and Ryker wondered what kind of criminal contacts Rudolf had.

Daria folded her arms over her chest as if to control her anger at her family for not supporting her decision. ''I'm innocent. I loved Fallon and Harry. I'm not going anywhere—especially not until we find their killer.''

"Look, I've done all I can—''

"And I appreciate it.''

"—but the police detectives now know that your sister not only left her share of the business to you, but that she had a five-million-dollar life insurance policy. Upon her death, the benefit went to you…''

"I know," Daria admitted, her voice sad. "We took out the policies so that if one of us died and the other inherited the business, the survivor would have enough cash to pay the estate tax on the business.''

"Your tax bill won't be anywhere near five million dollars," her father disagreed.

"We were thinking long-term. We didn't want to up the policy every time we expanded.''

"This won't work as a defensive strategy in court.''

Maybe her father was correct, maybe she should run while she still could.

"Tell her the rest," Shandra prodded.

"Joseph Ware's going to prosecute your case.''

The name meant nothing to Ryker, but Daria turned white. He pulled her against him to steady her and asked, "Who is Joseph Ware?''

Chapter Three

"Joseph Ware prosecuted that serial killer—the one dubbed the Baby Snatcher—last month," Daria told Ryker over a cup of tea at an all-night deli just down the street from her office. After she'd convinced her family to leave her to deal with her own troubles, she'd locked up the office, unable to even think about work.

And now Ryker expected her to take him to her home but, reluctant to allow him to invade her sanctuary, she'd suggested they stop for a bite to eat.

That she was unable to eat told her she was even more upset than she'd realized. The pecan pie didn't even tempt her. She couldn't eat even a cup of chicken noodle soup. Daria hated family confrontations, especially without her sister there to help buffer the antagonism.

Ryker sat across the table from her and bit into a massive corn beef sandwich on rye with extra mustard and sauerkraut. "So?"

"Ware takes on high-profile cases, and he doesn't ever lose."

"Everyone loses sometimes."

"Not him."

Ryker stabbed a pickle with a toothpick. "Okay, he's a top-notch D.A. So what? I'm sure you can afford a battery of high-priced attorneys to counter—"

"There's a personal history between our families."

"He's an ex-lover?"

Daria frowned at him. "Ware's my father's age. The two of them go way back and were once best friends. Apparently, they both fell in love with my mother."

"The friendship ended?"

"It turned into a hate fest." She set aside her tea. "Thirty years later there are still hard feelings between them, and that man would do anything to get back at my father, especially go after one of his children."

"I see."

"You don't have the entire picture yet. After my mother died, the vendetta escalated. I wouldn't put it past Ware to manufacture evidence against me to hurt my father." She hated to admit the truth, but she might as well let it out now. "And the only reason my father wants to help me is because he has to beat Ware."

His eyes pierced hers with sympathy. "You really believe that?"

"If you knew Rudy better, you'd believe it, too." She tightened her lips. "Fallon and I grew up in boarding schools and summer camps. We weren't part of family vacations or portraits. Before tonight, my father never visited a Harrington Bouquet store or my office. On the rare occasions when we can't avoid one another, he never inquires how the business is going.''

''Maybe he doesn't want to pry.''

She shook her head. ''He doesn't care. When my mother couldn't give him a son, my father divorced her when Fallon and I were five years old. Then Ware told her he didn't want used goods. She passed away a year after the split. Since the doctors could never find anything wrong with her, each man blames the other for her death. Fallon and I think she willed herself to die.''

''I'm sorry. I know what it's like to lose a mother. Mine died in a car accident.''

''How old were you?''

''Nine.''

She could read the pain in his eyes and reached across the table and squeezed his hand in an automatic gesture of comfort.

Touching him pleased her. She liked his quiet strength, the way he let her tell her story without interruptions.

Fallon had thought their mother's love for their father romantic. Daria had thought her mother foolish, and she'd vowed never to let a man mean more to her than her own life.

''Dad remarried when we were six years old, and Shandra immediately gave him the son he was waiting for. Fallon and I were prepared to hate Peter, the golden boy.'' She grinned. ''But how can anyone not like Peter?''

Ryker raised an eyebrow. ''He doesn't mind telling off the old man on your behalf, does he?''

''That's Peter, defender of all that's wrong in the world, but he also has nothing to lose. No matter what

Peter does, he's been groomed since birth to take over.''

''He's the sole heir to the Harrington conglomerate?'' Ryker guessed.

Daria and Fallon had never needed their father's money, thanks to their grandmother's trust fund and their own ingenuity. Still, the favoritism hurt. ''Dad's molding Peter to walk in his footsteps.''

''You don't sound envious.''

''Peter pays a price—a high one. Would you want to work with my father?''

Ryker raised his glass of milk to her before downing half in one giant gulp. ''Point taken.'' With his napkin he wiped his mouth. ''I grew up poor, and I'd watch the rich folks in town and imagine that they had perfect lives, but you didn't grow up with any more love in your life than I did.''

''I had Fallon.'' She swallowed the lump in her throat the size of a golf ball. ''What about your father?''

''He was an alcoholic who beat the crap out of me for no reason.'' She imagined a world of hurt that he was keeping to himself. ''I ran away from home at fifteen and joined the army.''

''Didn't they check your age?''

''Fake identification isn't hard to come by on the street. And I was big.''

''You didn't have sisters or brothers?''

''The military became my family.''

''And now?''

''Now I'm working for you.'' He reached for the check.

''I'll get that,'' she offered.

He grinned at her, that charming devil-may-care

grin that broke through her worries and made her realize he was a very handsome man who was about to spend the night in her apartment. "Don't worry, I'll add it to your bill."

"WOULD YOU MIND if we go back to the office?" Daria asked him as if she expected him to give her a hard time.

Ryker had no reason to argue. His job was to insert himself into her life, causing as little disruption as possible.

"Forget something?" he asked, helping her into her jacket in the nippy night air.

"I can pick up voice mail from home but, after the surprise visit from my parents, I forgot to pick up my secretary's messages. I guess the family visit distracted me more than I thought."

"No problem."

Was she stalling? Delaying his stay at her home? No matter, sooner or later she'd have to let him into her private life and he could be patient when necessary.

The short walk back to the office took only minutes. At this time of the evening the shops were all closed and the sidewalks much less crowded. Lovers strolled arm in arm and people walked their dogs.

Ryker looked down the street and Harrington Bouquet stood out like a beacon. "The lights inside the shop are still on." Thieves didn't announce their presence by turning on the lights. "Your employees—"

"Don't usually work this late." She strolled closer, peering through the glass panes of the storefront. "It's Peter and Elizabeth and…" Her voice rose an octave in shock. "They're kissing."

Her brother and the store manager? Not intruders. His heart rate calmed but adrenaline overload made him jumpy.

From her surprised tone and the look on Daria's face, she hadn't known about their relationship. And she didn't approve. His concern was that although there didn't appear to be any immediate danger, he still had the almost overwhelming urge to protect, to chase, to throttle an enemy.

"It's odd that neither of them has ever told me," she wondered aloud, her expression thoughtful as she unlocked the front door and entered the shop.

Ryker didn't like these kinds of surprises. Her brother's messing with the hired help sent alarm bells ringing. He filed away the facts to examine later. Right now, he wanted to concentrate on the explanations and crosscurrents of tension.

At their entrance, Peter and Elizabeth broke apart. Elizabeth raised her hand to the smudged lipstick on her mouth, clearly upset. Short, about five feet tall, with long dark hair and creamy white skin, she frowned at Ryker, then focused her attention on Daria.

Daria spoke in a voice that demanded an explanation. "Why are you two making out like kids in my store?"

"Because she's a very good kisser," Peter said teasingly. He placed his arm around Elizabeth and tugged her close. He seemed relaxed and happy, like a puppy dog caught chewing on a favorite slipper.

Elizabeth shrugged out from beneath Peter's arm, her face red. "I was just finishing up watering the plants. We got a little carried away. I didn't mean for you to learn…like this. I should have told you about us sooner.''

Elizabeth oozed sincerity and a little bit too much intensity. She'd been kissing Daria's brother, not robbing the place. And, apparently, they were both single adults. Neither wore a wedding ring, so why the big deal over a few smooches?

"Daria's a big girl," Peter said. "She'll get over our little surprise. Won't you, sis?"

Daria looked from Elizabeth to her brother, quite amazed. "You two are…"

"Hanging out." Peter finished the sentence with a playful grin. "If you have any objections, keep them to yourself."

Elizabeth elbowed Peter, but she faced Daria. "We didn't want you to find out this way."

"She didn't want you to find out *at all*," Peter added.

"Shut up," Elizabeth told him, her bright eyes on Daria. "We weren't hiding. I just thought you had enough on your mind right now."

Daria recovered quickly. "It's okay."

Peter's face lost the grin. "That's where you're wrong. It's more than okay. And now that you are aware of our relationship, I'd like you to think about giving Elizabeth a promotion."

"Peter!" Elizabeth shook her head, clearly exasperated and horrified.

Tension between brother and sister escalated. Daria kept her voice even. "Peter, you can date whoever you like, but stay out of my business."

Before her brother could say another word, Daria spun on her heel and walked out the door. Ryker followed, but not before he missed Elizabeth's sigh of disappointment or Peter's triumphant grin.

RYKER COULD SEE that as Daria unlocked her front door she tried to appear comfortable about letting him into her home, but she didn't quite succeed. After meeting her family he could almost understand her reluctance to invite anyone into her apartment.

The key clicked open the dead bolt, but she hesitated, then a crooked grin turned up one corner of her lips. "My place isn't exactly conventional."

He recalled her disgust with the one dusty chair in the living room that served as his office. Her address was one of the most exclusive in Manhattan, and her penthouse, with its own private elevator, had him prepared for luxurious European decadence filled with gilded antiques and Turkish carpets.

So when she opened the front door, a waft of fresh air scented with flowers was his first clue that she'd created something magical. The front hallway appeared to be a lush garden of tropical plants. He simply stared. Delicate white flowers bloomed among climbing green vines that arched over a lattice bower, hiding the ceiling and walls.

She ducked through the archway, and he followed her, amazed that anyone could turn their living space into a miniature Garden of Eden. Fountains bathed by soft lighting added to the junglelike effect, and a drawbridge actually took them over a goldfish pond where the plants reminded him of a wild English garden complete with reclining divans and Victorian coffee tables. Each room had a different atmosphere and different kinds of plants, revealing the tremendous thought, planning and design that had gone into the creation of her home.

When they reached a "clearing" with a hammock hung between two sturdy trees that arched upward to a vaulted ceiling of glass, he tilted back his head to be greeted by moonlight. Two beanbag chairs on either side of a stone table with a game of Go invited one to relax, rest or contemplate the universe. Stone statues peeked out between the plants, mixing art and nature's beauty with creature comforts.

"This is great. Awesome."

"I think so," she agreed.

While before now he hadn't been convinced of her innocence, he couldn't believe that anyone who had the spirit to create such beauty could be a murderer. His natural inclination was to discount her as a suspect but his training wouldn't let him. However, most likely, the murderer had come from Harry's past.

She turned to the right and they entered a landscaped area of bonsai trees, boulders, stepping-stones and manicured sand. "This is where I come to meditate." She pointed to a dark area with stone walls that had a cavelike appearance. "Over there is a whirlpool bath, steam room and sauna. I imported jungle plants from South America that like humidity and heat to decorate the hot zone."

The hot zone? "But it's cool in here."

"I have special ventilation and insulation systems."

Instead of artwork, she had imported exotic flowers. She'd selected a soft green carpet that reminded him of moss and made him want to kick off his shoes and go barefoot. He imagined her reading by the trickling brook lined with natural stones, dipping her fingers into the stream of water, her head pillowed by his chest.

She led him over a smooth pebble path through the Japanese garden, and into the central part of the penthouse, which was round and boasted a brick wall with a stove, oven and refrigerator. A wooden table with comfy-looking chairs sat on the polished wood floor. An herb garden hung in baskets around a picture window that looked out onto the city.

"Who takes care of all these plants?" he asked, in awe of the world she'd created in the center of Manhattan.

"I do. Elizabeth comes over once a week to help me. She calls it a labor of love, but now I'm wondering…"

"What?"

"If she's trying to work her way into the family by doing me favors."

"You don't like the idea of Peter and Elizabeth together?"

She shrugged. "Women are always after Peter for his money, but I never thought Elizabeth…"

"Did it ever occur to you that she genuinely likes your brother? You do."

"It just doesn't feel right. But I'll get over it."

A black cat with green eyes emerged from the bushes and brushed against her legs. She stooped to pick him up, scratched affectionately behind the ears. "Hi, Ace." She handed him a treat, then set him down on the floor where he ate the treat, then licked his paws clean. "Elizabeth is not just the manager of the New York store, she's my friend. She understands that I don't like strangers in my home and volunteered to water my plants when I get swamped and stuck at the office. Often I'd come home and she'd just be getting done and we'd talk over tea. Girl stuff. She's one of the few people I really trust. But she didn't trust me enough to tell me about her and Peter.''

''So she has a key to your home and the office?''

Daria nodded. ''We've known one another since college.''

''Did Elizabeth and Fallon get along?''

At his question, Daria spun to face him, her eyes wide in speculation. ''Strange that you should ask me that.''

''Why?''

''Fallon liked almost everyone, but…''

''She didn't like Elizabeth?'' he guessed.

''No, she didn't. But she could never tell me why—except that she claimed Elizabeth was sly.''

''Sly?''

''Elizabeth grew up poor. She went to school on scholarship, and she was always the outsider looking in.'' Ryker knew the feeling. He could recall how painful it was to pretend he didn't like sweets while he stood outside the local candy store waiting for his friends to buy an after-school treat. Daria continued in a sympathetic tone. ''Elizabeth couldn't afford to hang out with us at restaurants or buy the right clothes to fit in with our crowd, and she was too proud to accept loaners.''

''You sound like you admire her.''

''I do. Elizabeth worked harder than the rest of us because she had to. And she never complained about her circumstances.''

''What did Harry think about her?''

Daria shrugged. ''Harry always kept his opinions

to himself. He was a quiet man. Fallon talked non-stop. Probably why they got along so well.''

''They were happy?''

''Yes.'' Her voice was fierce, protective, sad. ''Fallon was quite proud of her marriage. Our parents didn't set much of an example.''

''How did Fallon get along with the rest of your family?''

Daria's hazel eyes turned defensive. ''You've met them.''

''And I have my opinion. I'd like yours.''

''Why?''

He held her gaze. ''Because someone could have framed you. Probably someone you know.''

Daria flinched as he made that statement. Clearly, she saw the logic to his words, but she didn't want to face the fact that someone she trusted had killed her sister and brother-in-law and then framed her for the murders.

Instead of answering his question, she walked away. ''Wait here. I'll get you a backup file.''

Obviously, she didn't want him in her office, or she needed a moment alone. He let her go, content to watch her silk-encased legs stroll across the room and down another hallway, knowing that she would return. He took a measure of comfort in the knowledge that she no longer seemed so uncomfortable about his presence in her home. Yet she had shut him out the moment he'd asked about her family. Although Daria and her folks weren't close, although she seemed to both resent and love them, she nevertheless protected their secrets.

Daria's half scream, half gasp from the direction of the back hallway had him racing after her, not even stopping to pull out the knife hidden in the sheath at his ankle. He should have checked the apartment before he'd allowed her inside. But he hadn't expected danger since he had no reason at all to believe anyone was after her.

And the decor had totally thrown him off guard. A mistake. He looked inside a bedroom, at least he assumed it was a bedroom, as it had a water bed surrounded by white flowering plants. The next room possessed a spectacular stained-glass window that overlooked a rose garden.

Where was she?

He rounded a corner. And bumped right into her. Automatically he grabbed her waist to steady her. "What's wrong?"

"The tapes are gone and the hard drive's wiped clean."

AFTER RECOVERING FROM the loss of her computer information, Daria made herself a cup of tea and handed Ryker a mug of coffee, more to steady her nerves and give her hands something to do than for any need of refreshment. Someone had invaded her home. Stolen her property. Her private sanctuary wasn't the safe haven she'd believed.

"Why didn't the police take the backup tapes?" Ryker asked.

"Daddy pulled some strings and the judge wouldn't give them a search warrant."

Cautiously Ryker sniffed the coffee.

Daria saw him hesitate. "It's okay. The beans were sealed. I just opened the bag."

"Right." He took a careful sip. "You want to call the cops and report a break-in?"

"I don't see the point. They won't believe me. And I don't want to give Ware an excuse to call me a liar in court. Besides, the chance of the police finding the person responsible doesn't seem likely."

"Unless the thief left fingerprints. While you were making refreshments, I phoned a friend. In the morning, he's going to deliver a kit so I can dust your office. He'll also bring over my equipment."

Daria took comfort from her tea, slightly uneasy to be sitting across her kitchen table from a stranger who was moving in with her. She didn't want to think about sharing her home with him, of the two of them spending nights together. "Is there any way to retrieve the information from my hard drive?"

"Not if they also reformatted the drive." Ryker leaned back in his chair, balancing on the rear legs. "However, I intend to contact your Internet service provider."

"What good will that do?"

"They have copies of your e-mail."

She hadn't known such a thing was possible. "That's the best news I've heard all night." Daria wasn't good with computers. Plants were her thing. She liked digging her fingers into the dirt. She liked watering, cutting and pruning. She liked talking to her flowers, too, but made a mental note to herself not to do that with a guest in her home. "But even if you retrieve my e-mails, that won't be enough to clear me, will it?"

"Probably not." Ryker got a strange look in his eyes and then he chuckled, bent and scooped Ace onto his lap. The cat must have been rubbing himself against Ryker's ankles and now he braced his back feet on Ryker's thighs, his front paws on his chest, and stared at him.

"Ace isn't accustomed to strangers. He's curious. My other two cats are hiding. He's the brave one."

Ryker let the cat sniff him, then slowly scratched behind Ace's ear. The cat accepted the petting, then leaped onto the floor and disappeared behind the wild sarsaparilla Daria had planted in the spring.

"Does Peter have a key?"

"No, but if he's been seeing Elizabeth... Surely you don't think my brother..."

Did he consider everyone she knew as a suspect? She supposed he did. She didn't even know if he believed in her innocence. Like the police, he considered the life insurance policy and Fallon's half of the business good motives. In fact, she'd give everything she had to bring back Fallon and Harry. Ryker's suspicions made dealing with her life more difficult. Especially when she was going to have to adopt his attitude. Damn it. She didn't like being suspicious of the people she trusted most. "Why do you ask?"

"I'm just getting a feel for your situation. What about your parents?"

"They don't have a key, but..."

"But what?"

"Fallon had one. And I'm not sure what happened to her personal effects. The police took her purse. My key is on her ring." Daria shuddered. "Whoever stole my computer out of the police evidence room could have a key to my apartment."

"We'll have the locks changed first thing tomorrow." Ryker frowned. "I'm surprised you don't have a security system, but then I suppose you don't have much to steal."

"You suppose right. Although some of these plants are extremely rare and expensive, they can't exactly be fenced at a pawnshop."

Daria realized that Ryker had been talking to her in a soothing voice. Obviously, he understood that having him stay in her apartment unnerved her. She wasn't accustomed to sharing her space. Especially not with a stranger.

Her face must have shown some of her thoughts because once again he tried to reassure her. "Relax. I won't attack you—"

"I didn't think you would."

"—however much I might like to." He grinned, that dashing grin that made her oh, so uncomfortable.

"I'm not in a joking mood."

"I wasn't joking." His eyes drilled her with intensity. "I find you attractive. And I've thought about kissing you from the moment you walked into my office."

So much for his reassuring and soothing her frazzled nerves. His direct approach caused her pulse to leap and a heat to kindle in her blood. "I'm not interested."

He chuckled, a sound rich, warm and almost tender. "You're entitled to your opinion. But there's an easy way to allay your anxiety."

"Is that so?" She didn't like him reading her so easily. Standing, she crossed her arms under her breasts and tried to stare him down. But as he rose to his feet, her gaze got caught in his magnetism, which was as dazzling as scarlet roses.

His grin challenged her. "You could just admit I'm irresistible. Kiss me and get it over with."

Chapter Four

"I hired you to find my sister's killer." Daria's words were meant to put Ryker in his place, to remind him that she was the employer and he the employee. If he thought she would fall for his charm on a dare, he'd learn better.

Daria had enough confidence in herself to recognize his challenge for what it was—a juvenile attempt to provoke her into doing something she didn't wish to do. She didn't need to prove anything to him, or to herself for that matter.

She had no intention of kissing him. She had no intention of starting any kind of relationship with a man who lived with electronic equipment for companionship. He'd had no pets in that dusty place he'd called home, not even *one* plant. He had no pictures on the walls. Between her observations and what Harry's attorney had told her about Ryker Stevens she'd concluded that his heart was as cold as the circuit boards he'd dumped on the floor and as empty as his bare walls.

She had no interest—okay, almost no interest—in kissing a man who lived the way he did. However, she wouldn't be a living, breathing female if she didn't have a smidgen of curiosity. The man was quite the hunk. And there was much more to him than rugged good looks.

But even if he found Fallon and Harry's killer and she proved her innocence, she didn't need the kind of heartache getting involved with a loner like Ryker would inevitably bring. Her attorney had warned her that Ryker was excellent at what he did, but he was also the sailor with a woman in every port. A man who would say goodbye without looking back.

If she'd wanted a fling, Ryker might be perfect man material. With his athletic body and intelligent mind, she suspected he'd be sexy in bed and easy to talk to afterward, but she didn't want a fling. She didn't even want to complicate her life with a relationship right now—but if she did, she'd want a man who could do long-term.

"Jail is no place for a woman like you," he agreed too easily with her last statement. "You need your creature comforts. Your plants. Your pets. Pampering. I'd be more than willing to indulge you."

His eyes twinkled with mischief, as if he fully realized how outrageous he sounded and was waiting for her to tell him off. She didn't like him toying with her, but she wouldn't give him the satisfaction of an emotional response.

"The guest bedroom is in there. Make yourself at home." She pointed down the hall, then walked away from him in the opposite direction. "Good night."

"Sweet dreams."

She ignored him and forced herself to maintain a

normal walking pace, but she wanted to run. Especially after his words followed her to her room, lingering in her mind like a dreamy temptation.

He wanted to *indulge* her? What exactly did that mean and why did just thinking about him make her think about kissing in the starlight and breakfast in bed?

Ruthlessly, she shoved away an image of those strong hands skimming her flesh. If he wanted to indulge her then he could earn his money and figure out who'd murdered Fallon and Harry.

Daria shut her bedroom door. None of the interior doors in her apartment had locks. She wasn't in the habit of inviting strangers into her home. Any rare guest she invited would respect a closed door. However, Ryker didn't resemble her other visitors.

He was brash. Bold. Larger-than-life. He was a man accustomed to plain speech and pursuing his objectives. And yet she had the distinct impression that he was deliberately pressing her buttons, testing her, categorizing her reactions for his own reasons. He was intelligent enough to know she wasn't interested in him, yet he had his own agenda.

Perhaps she should fire him. However, Harry's attorney had respected Ryker Stevens's abilities, and her brother-in-law would have chosen his attorney carefully. Harry hadn't been impressed easily. Oddly, she didn't feel threatened by Ryker's honest advances—no matter how brazen they'd been. Deep down, the feminine part of her was flattered that Ryker would even bother. She imagined he normally pursued women who weren't quite as particular as she, women who might enjoy a one-night man.

In theory, Daria had no problem with two adults taking pleasure in one another's bodies, then never seeing each other again. But that kind of fling had never interested her. Perhaps preserving the propriety of the Harrington name affected her more than she would have liked. But long ago she'd ceased trying to win her father's approval. Her choices in men were her own.

She picked educated men, businessmen, in the hopes of someday finding a soul mate. An ex-military man like Ryker, one step up from a mercenary soldier, was outside her experience. It wasn't that she considered him beneath her socially, he simply came from a different world. The chances of the two of them meshing in any kind of meaningful way were zilch, zero, zip.

Still, as she finished brushing her teeth, turned out the bathroom light and then snuggled into the warmth of her water bed, she wondered if she was a snob. If Ryker had been a college professor or a stockbroker would she have encouraged his advances?

She shivered at the memory of his tantalizing promise to "indulge her." What exactly had he meant by that delicious-sounding statement? Ryker Stevens didn't seem like the kind of man to make a promise without the ability to follow through. He appeared quite sure he could get copies of her e-mails from her Internet service provider. And he'd seemed just as sure that he could show her a good time.

Fallon would have told her to take a few chances.

Although her sister was no longer here, Daria knew
Fallon would be shocked and pleased that she'd
agreed to let a stranger spend a few nights in her
home.

Daria hoped she hadn't made a mistake. She tossed
and turned, disturbing Ace, who moved to a far corner
of the bed. How could she sleep with Ryker in her
home?

Ace purred softly, then snoozed. The cat didn't always sleep with her, but tonight he must have sensed
she was a bit unnerved by the man just down the hall.

Daria realized she'd never sleep if she kept thinking about Ryker. So instead she went over the mystery of who could have stolen her backup tapes.
Everyone who worked at Harrington Bouquet's head-
quarters had access to her purse and her keys. She
kept her keys in her purse, which hung on a hook
behind her office door during the day. If she attended
a meeting in the conference room or used the rest
room, she usually left her purse behind, a habit she
would alter after Ryker changed her apartment's locks
tomorrow.

Her telephone rang.

Daria jumped. Who could be calling this late? She
rolled over in bed and picked up the receiver.
"Hello?"

"Sorry to phone so late, but you didn't answer any
of my calls to the office."

"Mike?"

Mike Brannigan was the chief operating officer of
a company interested in acquiring Harrington Bouquet. They'd dated a few times and she'd given him

her unlisted phone number. She'd stopped seeing him after she'd realized that he'd been as interested in acquiring Harrington Bouquet for his company as he had been in her. She hadn't wanted to sell the company then, and she wasn't interested in doing so now.

His firm voice zipped through the wires with the energy she always associated with him. "I just want you to know that my offer still stands."

She almost told him no again, but if she and Ryker didn't succeed, she could be facing the rest of her life in a jail cell. Perhaps she shouldn't be too hasty in making her decision.

"Mike, I appreciate the call. If I put the business on the market, you'll be the first to know."

Daria hung up the phone, knowing Mike Brannigan needed to be added to her list of suspects. He'd had access to her purse, and he wanted Harrington Bouquet. Tomorrow, she'd have to tell Ryker about Mike. She wondered if the invasion of her privacy would ever end.

At the soft knock on her door, she jumped again. "Yes?"

Ryker took her response as an invitation to enter. "I heard the phone ring. Is everything okay?"

"EVERYTHING'S FINE. Good night."

Daria clearly meant to dismiss him, but Ryker didn't retreat from her bedroom. Here she had more potted plants that he didn't recognize, delicate-leafed greenery with tiny white blooms that scented the air but didn't overpower. The blanket on her bed looked Indian in design and the floor lamp beside her had a stem of silver and black glass that swept upward into a spiral of swirling color. Her taste was unique, eclectic and homey.

But there was nothing homey about the lacy gold negligee that exposed her creamy shoulders and skimmed the swell of her breasts. Not only did the negligee allow her skin to play peekaboo with his fantasies, the sexy garment revealed a side of her she probably didn't want him to see.

"You sure you don't need anything from me?" he teased her, hoping she would blush, but when she didn't, he took pride in her attitude. The lady might value her privacy, but she had grit in spades.

As if she wasn't mostly undressed between silk sheets, her tone was prim, proper. "Look, I appreciate your concern, but if I need you, I'll let you know."

"Do you always do that?"

"What?"

"Attack when you feel defensive?"

She rolled her eyes heavenward. "You call that an attack?"

"You implied you had no need for me. That's a put-down."

"I didn't realize you had such a fragile ego."

He grinned. "Another put-down."

"You're being deliberately obtuse. Stalling. I'd like you to go now."

He ignored her request. Since she wasn't volunteering information, she forced him to pry. "Who called?"

"It's a private matter."

"Look, everyone you talk to is my concern. Every

business deal, every phone call, every contact you have with another human being is my business until we find Fallon and Harry's killer.''

As he spoke, she yanked the blanket up, then folded her arms over it to keep it in place. She glared daggers at him. And then she spoke one word. ''Okay.''

Had she actually agreed with him?

The lady was full of surprises. Clearly she didn't like telling him about her personal life, but she saw the necessity. He sat at the foot of her water bed next to the cat, tried not to think how the undulations caused them both to rock and waited for her to organize her thoughts.

He didn't mind the wait. He'd never seen a woman look so fragile and strong at the same time. With her hair tousled and the makeup washed from her face, she appeared more vulnerable and younger than earlier—until she came to some kind of decision, indicated by the angle of her chin and the determination in her hazel eyes.

''The phone call was from Mike Brannigan.''

''Of Brannigan Industries?''

She nodded. ''He wanted to let me know that he's still interested in buying Harrington Bouquet.'' She held his gaze, then looked away as if there was more that she didn't want to tell him.

''How long since he first approached you about buying your company?''

''Six months. He thinks the floral boutiques will fit in with their corporation's high-end chocolate shops and extravagant jewelry stores. They also have some floral shops in large hotels and think Harrington Bouquet will upgrade their image.''

Ryker didn't want to pry, but he needed answers. ''Does Brannigan have a key to your office or apartment?''

''I never gave him a key. But we went out to dinner a few times.''

''So he had access to your purse?''

''I'm afraid so. But he would have no motive to plant poison in the coffee I served my sister.''

''Of course he would. With Fallon dead and you in jail, you may have to sell Harrington Bouquet.''

''Mike Brannigan, a Princeton graduate with a Harvard law degree, set me up for murder so he could buy Harrington Bouquet? Don't you think that sounds a little far-fetched?''

''Can you think of any scheme that includes framing you and poisoning Fallon and Harry that *isn't* far-fetched?''

She sighed. ''You're just full of good cheer. Am I going to have to suspect all my friends, family and business acquaintances?''

''Probably. Once my computer equipment arrives in the morning, I'll start to narrow down the list.''

''How?''

''By looking into your acquaintances' backgrounds to find out if any have criminal records.'' At the frown on Daria's face, he knew he had struck a sensitive nerve. ''What?''

''Nothing.''

''I thought we agreed you wouldn't hold out on me.''

"She can't have anything to do with…"

"Who is *she*?"

"I'm a Big Sister to a young girl named Tanya Johnson." He recognized the program that paired troubled kids from broken homes with volunteers who took an interest in the children. "We do things together once a week. In the summer, she works in the New York store. She's fourteen and has a criminal record. And she would have absolutely no motive to frame me—although she does have this interest in poisons."

From her tone she felt protective about the kid, another admirable trait. "What kind of police record?"

"Drugs. Prostitution."

"What do you mean she's into poisons?"

"When we first met, I tried to teach her how the stuff she ingested would kill her just like poisons in some of my plants. I figured if she understood what the chemicals were doing to her, it might help her fight the addiction. She's been clean for a while now. And she's fascinated by my plants. I thought she might work full-time for me one day…"

"Tell me more about her interest in poisons," he prodded.

Daria shrugged and the blanket slipped a little. "You know how kids are. Death fascinates Tanya. Maybe it's because when she was three years old the social workers didn't find her until several days after her mother died. I think she takes comfort in knowing that if life gets too tough she can end it."

"You're saying she's suicidal?"

"I'm saying her life is tough. She has no family and some learning disabilities."

"What kind?"

"ADHD. Attention deficit hyperactivity disorder. She's very smart, but she's hyper and has a short attention span."

"Is she violent?"

"Not anymore. Not since she kicked the drugs."

"So Tanya had access to the keys in your purse, and she's familiar with the poison flower that—"

"Yes. But she has no reason—"

"Maybe she was jealous of your relationship with your sister."

"Tanya never liked Fallon. She was jealous of how close I was to my sister but the idea that she would kill her is outrageous."

"Who knows what goes through the mind of an ex-addict."

"Do you realize that in just a few hours you've named as suspects my parents, my brother, my friend Elizabeth and now Tanya?"

"And Mike Brannigan. Maybe him most of all."

"Why?"

"He's smart. Whoever planned this was meticulous and cunning." Ryker thought hard. "Tell me, of all our suspects, which of them knows that you don't drink coffee?"

"All of them. But none knew that I saved the Jamaican Blue Mountain for Fallon."

"That could be irrelevant."

"What do you mean?"

"Well, if someone wanted to frame you, they might not care who you killed."

"You mean that they might not have deliberately planned for me to kill my sister?"

"It's possible. And so is the reverse. We need to look at Fallon's and Harry's enemies. Maybe someone wanted to kill them and you just got used."

THE FOLLOWING MORNING Daria awakened to the aroma of frying bacon and perking coffee.

Last night Ace, the traitor, had departed with Ryker, leaving her to toss and turn alone in her bed. When she'd finally fallen asleep, she'd slept deeply and still felt a tad groggy.

A shower woke her fully. She dressed with more care than usual, picking out a green blouse, long gray skirt and soft kid boots. She French-braided her hair, skillfully weaving in a few sprigs of jasmine.

When she entered the kitchen, Ryker was in the process of transferring crisp bacon from the frying pan to a plate. Wearing jeans and a sexy white T-shirt, he looked comfortable in front of the stove.

When he saw her he gestured to a chair. "Morning."

"You've been busy."

She took a seat and placed a napkin on her lap. He'd squeezed fresh orange juice and with a spatula removed an omelette from a pan and placed it on a plate before her.

"I'm an early riser. My clothes and equipment were delivered earlier. There were no prints on your computer or keyboard."

"Not even mine?"

"Nope. Someone was very careful and wiped it clean." He poured her tea and himself coffee, then sat across the table from her and dug into his eggs.

Usually, she skipped food in the morning and just read the paper over a cup of tea, but the food smelled so good that she opted to eat breakfast.

She took a bite of the omelette and delicate flavors assaulted her taste buds. "You can cook for me anytime."

He grinned and passed her the bacon. "You're so good to me."

She swallowed and wiped her mouth. "I thought I heard banging while I was in the shower."

"You did. The locksmith has come and gone." He dug into the back pocket of his jeans and handed her a key on a string. "Wear this around your neck."

Daria sipped her orange juice, noting that the command in his tone didn't allow for any argument. Between bites of omelette, she spoke, "Elizabeth needs a key to get in and take care of my plants and so does my cleaning lady."

He added sugar and cream to his coffee. "Can that wait a day or two?"

"Why?"

He stirred the coffee, sipped, then added more sugar. "I'm installing a security system. It'll take a key and a code to get inside. With the system I have in mind, each person will have their own code, including you."

"Okay."

He eyed her thoughtfully over the brim of his cup.

"You're agreeable this morning. Do you always wake up in such a good mood?"

When a handsome man cooked her breakfast? *Yes.* With her favorite Western omelette prepared just the way she liked it? *Oh yes.* There was just something sexy about eating food he'd prepared for her. Something homey about sharing breakfast and conversation instead of running out the door.

However, she had no intention of sharing her thoughts. Last night she'd known he'd been teasing her when he'd come to her bedroom, but he'd also been testing her resolve. In some ways she'd felt threatened by his invasion of her privacy, but in other ways she'd felt comfortable sharing her problems as well as her private space.

Daria knew she spent too much of her downtime alone. But when she forced herself to go out, she often couldn't wait to shed her date and retreat to her penthouse. The thought of allowing a man to come here usually never entered her head.

Ryker's presence didn't seem like an invasion. He fit in. As he fed a piece of bacon to Ace, she realized that even her persnickety cat liked him, although the other two had yet to come out of hiding.

Just because the man could cook didn't mean she considered him compatible as a lover. No man she'd ever dated would have come into her room without an invitation—or refused to leave. But, while she'd been slightly uncomfortable, she'd also felt more alive than she had in a long time.

Fear never entered the picture. The man had too much cool control over himself to cross certain boundaries, but clearly he drew the line in a different place than she did.

She washed down the last of her egg with a sip of tea. "What's today's agenda?"

"You tell me." He eyed the last slice of bacon on her plate. "What's your routine?"

She offered him the bacon. "I go to work."

"Then that's what we do." Using his fingers, he plucked the piece from her plate and finished it in three bites. "I want to assess your books, meet your employees, get a handle on the flow of traffic in your office."

"Sounds good." She eyed his clothes, totally unsuitable for the office, and wondered if he even owned a suit.

As if reading her thoughts, he raised an eyebrow. "Along with my equipment, I brought over business attire."

She frowned at him. "Are my thoughts that obvious?"

"Yes." Then he winked at her. "That's why I'm so positive that you find me charming."

"Really?"

"And irresistible."

"If you're so irresistible, then why did I send you away last night?"

"Because you're fighting yourself."

"Do you always live in a fantasy world?" she countered with a shake of her head.

He chuckled. "You're doing it again. Attacking when you feel defensive."

The man was utterly impossible. She didn't need

his pop psychology, she needed answers to who'd laced the coffee in her office with poison and who'd stolen her backup tapes and wiped her hard drive clean. "Look, could we stick to talking about my case?"

His eyes twinkled. "Only if you stop looking at me like a sex object."

"I do no such thing."

"Right. Then how come you were staring at me like a woman starved for a man?"

"The *food* smelled good. I was hungry. And you're really out there, way off base, you know that?"

He didn't say a word, he just shook his head with that superior smirk of his that raised her blood pressure. She'd attacked him again, and no doubt he thought she was being defensive, but what woman wouldn't be? The man had an ego the size of the Empire State Building.

She almost retreated to her room and left the dishes to him, but fair was fair, he'd cooked, she'd clean up. "Why don't you change, and I'll load the dishwasher."

"Yes, ma'am. Mind if I finish my coffee first?"

"Take it with you."

He rose to his feet. "Is there a hurry?"

She scraped the plates and placed them in the dishwasher. "I don't like to be late."

He sat back down. "Today should be the exception."

"Why?"

"Because if you're going to introduce me as your

new lover and in-house accountant, we want people to speculate about us.''

She could tell he was enjoying himself. Damn the man. He intended for them to come in late so her employees would believe they'd spent the night making love.

And she'd agreed to this crazy plan.

What she hadn't counted on was the awkward flutter in her stomach. Playacting should have been easy. But there was nothing easy about pretending to be his lover—because he'd been right earlier. She *was* fighting an attraction to him.

Chapter Five

Ryker changed into one of the Armani suits that Logan Kincaid had insisted he include in his wardrobe during a mission to protect a Saudi prince. The Shey Group paid Ryker very well, and he could easily afford designer clothes. Since he'd socked away approximately ninety percent of his pay over the last five years and had invested wisely, Ryker didn't need to work at all. But acquiring material objects had never been important to him. Neither were clothes. Although he saw the logic of wearing suits that allowed him to fit in, he'd resented buying a designer wardrobe that he didn't want and shoes that cost enough to pay a family's food bill for several months.

But the look of surprise on Daria's face when he reappeared in her kitchen was worth every penny he'd paid. Her jaw actually dropped, and he would have sworn that for a second she'd stopped breathing.

"Do the clothes make the man?" he teased.

"The clothes show off the shoulders," she teased right back. "I figured you worked at home in jeans."

"You figured I couldn't afford these threads," he countered.

"Not true." She picked up her purse and led the way to the front door. "With what I'm paying you, you can afford to wear Presidential Platinum Rolex watches on both wrists and diamond rings on your toes."

He locked the door behind them, then enjoyed watching her drive smoothly through the traffic to her office. He would have liked to bring his computer system along, but he didn't want anyone asking questions about his fancy hardware. For now, he'd make do with whatever systems she had and upgrade later if necessary.

They arrived through her private entrance they'd used before, bypassing the busy boutique on the ground floor, which fronted Fifth Avenue. Daria walked through the hall with quick steps, her boot heels clicking on the tile, a sound he found both provocative and irritating.

"This floor consists of my office, which you've already seen. My secretary, Jeanie Banks, works in the area outside my office."

"So to lace the coffee with poison, someone would have to get past Jeanie?"

"Not necessarily. She frequently leaves on errands, and I often work late, Jeanie has kids to pick up from day care by six."

Jeanie, a tall, slender woman with curly brown hair, started to greet Daria, then did a double take when she noticed Ryker holding Daria's hand. Much too polite to make a comment, her eyebrows nevertheless raised, drawing attention to her pierced eyebrow.

Daria stopped at Jeanie's desk and picked up a

stack of messages. ''Jeanie, this is Ryker Stevens, our new accountant.''

''Pleased to meet you.'' Jeanie gave him the once-over and her lips melted into a grin she couldn't keep back. ''Very pleased.''

From here Ryker could see the conference room, a unisex rest room and four other offices, one of which had been turned into a kitchen. Besides her secretary, Daria employed a full-time bookkeeper, a purchasing agent and a customer service specialist who also doubled as a floral designer. Down a floor was construction, real estate development, and advertising and marketing.

Either Jeanie was the most inefficient secretary he'd ever met, or she needed more help. Papers in need of filing sat piled on her desk, trickled over the edge and puddled in a two-foot stack on the floor. Four phone lines had the lights lit up, and Jeanie actually had one message pinned to her blouse.

''Oh, I almost forgot.'' She tugged the message free and handed the note to Daria. ''This one's important.''

''What?''

''It's from one of our greenhouse growers in Brazil. He sounded frantic, but said he'd be out of touch for the next hour.''

''I'll take care of it.'' Daria clutched the note in her hand, clearly needing to make her phone call. ''I'll introduce Ryker to everyone, then call him back.''

Daria's overworked purchasing agent, Isabelle White, an African-American woman in her sixties, looked just as busy and harried as Daria's secretary. Isabelle hung up the phone just as Daria knocked, and Ryker followed her into the office. Apparently Isabelle liked plants, too, but unlike Daria, who was careful not to overwhelm the senses with too much scent, Isabelle's office reeked with a blatant floral mixture that had knockout potential.

He breathed through his mouth, but Daria didn't seem to mind. She appeared to be more concerned with Isabelle's reaction to meeting him. "I've hired us an accountant. Ryker Stevens will smooth out our operations."

"Pleased to meet you." She sounded anything but pleased and eyed him suspiciously.

Isabelle stood, showing off a floral-print dress that hugged her curves and emphasized her large chest. She plunged right into what was bothering her. "You think we're spending too much money on our exotic blooms? Well, we are. But I can't match the quality anywhere else and—"

"Isabelle, relax." Daria hugged the supercharged woman. "I know you squeeze the best prices out of our suppliers. Ryker's here to help with the paperwork, not look over your shoulder."

"Good." The woman's eyes flashed a warning as she eyed him up and down. "I've been with the girls since they opened shop, and I don't take kindly to interference. From anyone."

Isabelle was defending her territory like a pit bull. If she'd noticed Ryker's hand on Daria's arm as they'd entered, she hadn't reacted one way or another.

"But Daria is working too hard and we could use

help around here.'' Isabelle stared at him like a mother hen. ''If you know what's good for you, you'll treat my girl right.''

''I have every intention of treating her right,'' Ryker agreed, deliberately making his voice husky so she couldn't miss the innuendo. He almost chuckled as Daria stiffened and Isabelle's brown eyes widened.

The older woman didn't hesitate to speak her mind. ''What's going on here?''

''Ryker and I…'' Daria looked at him, flustered. She could have won an Academy Award for the embarrassed act—except he suspected she really was embarrassed, which he found rather cute.

So he felt obligated to help Daria out before she blew his cover. ''We're involved.''

Isabelle didn't say another word. She simply crossed her arms over her chest, closed her mouth, sat behind her desk with a thump and gave Daria a we-*will*-talk-later look that he fully intended to eavesdrop on.

Meanwhile, Ryker did his best to restrain a chuckle. He hadn't enjoyed a mission this much in a very long time. Inserting himself into Daria's world was fun and reminded him how much he loved his job. Constant challenges. Freedom. Not to mention the teamwork with some of the most skilled and loyal guys around. He knew he could call the Shey Group team members in to help at any time.

Right now he needed to assess the situation and lay out the groundwork. Once he came up with a plan, he'd contact Logan and bring in the other guys as needed.

Daria escorted Ryker from Isabelle's office, clearly trying to cover her unease at their "relationship" by talking business. "My customer service specialist/floral designer is gone for the day. Cindy Parks's scoping out a hotel ballroom and doing a final consult with Selena Diaz for her wedding to Brad Morrison next month."

Daria spoke the name of the Spanish singing sensation and her movie-star heartthrob with the ease of someone accustomed to dealing with celebrities. He imagined her client list was the envy of her competitors.

Daria opened the last door at the end of the hall. "And in here is Sam Watkins, my bookkeeper."

Sam's tiny office had no window but lots of plants. Since his head didn't clear the monitor on his desk, Ryker estimated the man's height at around five feet five inches. He was maybe twenty-two. With thick-framed glasses chipped in one lens, Sam appeared every inch the nerdy bookkeeper. He didn't even look up as they entered.

"Sam, I'd like you to meet Ryker Stevens, our new accountant."

Ryker wondered if the bookkeeper might feel threatened as Isabelle had, but if Sam resented Ryker, he didn't show it. In fact, Ryker couldn't be sure the kid who stared at his computer screen with such intense concentration had even let Daria's words register.

Sam nodded once to acknowledge them, then started typing furiously.

"Perhaps we could come back later," Ryker suggested.

He expected Daria to agree. Instead, she walked behind Sam's chair, placed her hands on his shoulders and massaged his neck in a sisterly manner. "Did you pull another all-nighter?"

"Had to. Exams. Next week."

"Sam's working his way through night college," she explained to Ryker then directed her attention to Sam. "Have you had breakfast or, for that matter, did you have any dinner last night?"

Ryker wasn't sure he liked Daria rubbing the kid's shoulders, sisterly manner or not. He forcibly relaxed his own tense muscles. Daria might be particular about whom she dated, but she certainly cared about her employees. Isabelle White had been ready to defend her boss. Jeanie clearly liked her. When Sam stopped typing and glanced up at Daria, he had puppy-dog adoration in his eyes.

Sam blinked. "Forgot to eat again."

Daria sighed. "I want you to leave right now."

"But—"

"Take the rest of the day off. Eat and get some sleep."

Sam gestured to a stack of papers. "The bills?"

"Ryker will see to it." Daria flicked off the computer monitor. "Go."

"Okay. Okay. Sheesh. I'm out of here." Sam pushed the glasses that had slipped down his nose back up onto the bridge. "And thanks."

After Sam scooted out the door, Ryker flicked the monitor back on. "Are your computers networked?"

"Yes. Why?"

"It'll make my job easier."

Ryker slid into Sam's chair knowing Daria wouldn't rub *his* shoulders. He'd expected her to be a competent businesswoman. What he hadn't expected was the care she gave to every element of her life. The guest room he'd slept in possessed more creature comforts than he had at home—a television, an alarm clock, even a fluffy terry-cloth robe. She'd stocked the bathroom with a basket filled with toiletries like dental floss and different shampoos in travel sizes, and he'd found a brand-new toothbrush waiting in the medicine cabinet, fresh towels hanging on the racks.

She pampered her guests, and she took care of her employees. While each office reflected the occupant's own preferences, the furniture was new, the chairs plush and comfortable and the lighting good. Framed prints hung on papered walls with coordinating plants in planters and pots. The office didn't so much look decorated as friendly and comfortable.

Ryker glanced at the program Sam had been using. Expenses, salaries and sales were clearly broken down for each store. "The kid knows his stuff."

Daria peeked over Ryker's shoulder, her warm breath stroking his cheek. "In another year, Sam's going to be a CPA. I'll be lucky if he'll agree to work for me full-time." She straightened and headed out of the office. "I'll leave you to my bills. If you have any questions, ask Isabelle."

"Isabelle?"

"She used to do the books before I hired Sam. She

gave up the job when we bought the computer system, so she might not be that helpful after all."

"Isabelle's not good on a computer?"

Daria grinned. "She claims they were created by the devil to test our souls."

"Then I doubt she has the ability to have altered your e-mail."

"Good point. At least I can trust someone around here." Daria's tone was sarcastic.

He drilled her with a stare. "You can trust me, Daria."

"Can I?" She searched his face, looking for something, but he hadn't a clue what.

He sought to reassure her. "I always keep my promises."

"Trouble is, you haven't really made any, have you?"

TWO HOURS LATER, Ryker had a much clearer picture of Harrington Bouquet's operations. As far as cash flow, the company was in great shape. Despite the incredible speed of their expansion, the stores turned an immediate profit after opening due to a worldwide clientele of wealthy customers who appreciated buying exotic flowers that couldn't be purchased from other florists.

Daria offered several stunning species that had originally been found wild in Africa and Brazil. She'd cornered the market by cultivating the wild specimens in huge greenhouses that she owned; then she shipped the rare flowers worldwide. Harrington Bouquet was the only florist to offer Thundercloud Roses or Pink

Snowflakes. Passion Perfect flowers, which came in a variety of colors, sizes and shapes, were all the rage, expensive and marketed mostly to the rich and famous.

In addition, the flowers could be ordered to arrive in vases of hand-blown Venetian glass, delicate gold-filigreed cachepots or custom-cut marble urns. Each Harrington Bouquet store had weekly standing orders to deliver fresh flowers to the homes and hotel suites of movie stars, the offices of the movers and shakers in many of the world's capitals and even the cabins of ocean-going and luxury yachts when in port.

The company had even expanded into construction, flying their own team of workers to different cities to open the stores to Daria's exacting requirements. Like Tiffany's, the stores weren't selling just product, but service, exclusivity and brand name.

The hefty cash profits that resulted from this strategy had left the company ripe to go public, if the owners wished to cash out. No wonder Mike Brannigan wanted to buy the business.

Ryker had known that Daria Harrington was wealthy the moment she'd stepped into his apartment, but he'd never have guessed that she and her sister had become so extraordinarily successful. He wondered how many other people knew the company's financial strength and whether that success had anything to do with Fallon's and Harry's murders.

Daria had never mentioned whether she knew what Harry Levine did for a living. His wife's travels had been a perfect cover for the CIA operative, and a real possibility existed that an enemy of Harry's had gotten to him through Daria. Logan Kincaid had the connections to find out about Harry's last agency assignment, and Ryker made a note to send an encrypted e-mail to his boss from his own computer system with questions.

Meanwhile, Ryker dug deeper into Daria's computer network and learned that any kid could have hacked into her system. She had twenty-four-hour hard connections to the Internet and only basic firewalls.

A quick peek into her operating system told him that she updated her antivirus protection system regularly. But he knew how an expert could have hacked past the firewall into her system. He shut the remaining back doors, but his effort was like closing the barn door after the cows had escaped. The damage was already done. The trick would be to see if he could isolate the worm that had allowed the hacker access to alter her e-mails and discover who had caused the problem.

Ryker was in the middle of tracking down several possibilities when Isabelle knocked on his door and then entered. Isabelle didn't wait to take a seat before she started talking. "She could use your help right about now."

"She?" He saved his work and cleared his screen before facing Isabelle. "Daria? What's wrong?"

"The evil one is back in her office."

"The evil one?"

"Shandra Harrington."

Daria's stepmother had returned without her husband? And just why did Isabelle believe that Shandra was evil or that Daria needed help? It occurred to him that Isabelle might be lying or exaggerating. She could want him to leave his office so she could snoop around and see what he'd been up to. But even an expert wouldn't be able to find a crack in the software now.

Supposedly Isabelle didn't like computers, but that would be a convenient story to give out if she wanted to hide the damage she'd done. But Isabelle had been with the firm for years. It was unlikely she'd have kept her computer skills a secret for all that time if she really did have them. Most likely, the woman was exactly what she seemed, Daria's friend and mother figure who knew how the company worked from the inside out. Isabelle knew where the loyalties lay, where the bodies were buried. And if Isabelle thought Daria needed help, then he was wasting time here when he could be with Daria.

He came around his desk. "Thanks for giving me a heads-up. I'll see what I can do."

"YOUR FATHER'S TURNED into a tightwad," Shandra complained in the thick Boston accent that always seemed affected to Daria—as if Shandra wanted to remind the world that her ancestors went back to the *Mayflower*. While Shandra hadn't been a good step-mother, she hadn't been so bad either. Shandra hadn't hit them or deprived them of material things. She was never deliberately cruel. She'd simply washed her hands of her stepchildren to concentrate on pleasing their father. Even Peter took a back seat to Rudolf. The woman was the epitome of shallow and spent her days going from her personal trainer to her cosmetologist to her dress designer.

Daria had to give her credit. Shandra loved Rudy Harrington. She didn't just love his money or the power he could command, Shandra loved Daria's father with her entire heart and soul and lived to win his approval, hence her pathetic attempts at age fifty to look as if she was still twenty. Of course, Daddy didn't fully approve of anyone except Peter, so Shandra had set herself an impossible task.

Daria wished the woman would leave her alone. Two visits in one week was unprecedented. With a possible murder charge hanging over her head, Daria didn't have time for petty marital squabbles right now. She had an urgent phone call to return from her main warehouse supplier in South America, several messages from her attorney and a hundred day-to-day details of running Harrington Bouquet to take care of.

But Shandra looked as if she was about to come unglued. Her mascara had run, forming dark smudges under her eyes, and her lips quivered with tension. Still, Daria couldn't quite buy her act. She knew Shandra could turn on the tears like a spigot.

The woman had never before asked for her help either, so obviously she believed this marital spat was important. Daria tried to make her voice kind. "Maybe you're spending too much money."

"No more than usual." Shandra removed a lace hankie from her purse and twisted it between her manicured fingers.

"The stock market's down, and Dad doesn't like to dip into his capital." Even in retirement, her father would live off dividends and interest, preserving the principal he considered sacrosanct. She knew how her father managed money because while Rudy might not have been a loving father, he'd taught his daughters how to administer their trust fund. He'd also been furious when his daughters had dipped into the capital to start Harrington Bouquet, but that was best forgotten.

"Rudy even told Peter he couldn't buy that new Jag, and you know he never denies *Peter* anything."

"Maybe Dad's tightening the purse strings to force Peter to take on some fiscal responsibility."

Daria couched her words with care. She had no doubt that every word she uttered would be repeated verbatim to her father. Although she had long ago given up trying to please the man, she saw no point in antagonizing him either. And besides, Shandra might repeat this conversation in front of Peter, and Daria didn't want to hurt her brother.

Shandra dabbed her eyes with her handkerchief. "Something's wrong. Rudy let Boris go."

The butler? The news startled Daria, but didn't overly concern her. She considered having a butler to open the door and lay out clothes an affectation. "Boris must be nearing eighty. Don't you think it's time he retired?"

"But we didn't *replace* him."

"You know how particular Dad is about who works in his home." Father and daughter were alike that way. "Boris has been his butler for forty years. It may take time to replace him."

A knock on the door followed by Ryker's entrance

didn't surprise Daria. All morning she'd been overly aware of him working down the hall, wondering when she would see him.

When Ryker entered, even Shandra seemed to notice how terrifically his shoulders filled out his suit jacket. He strode over to Daria and brushed her lips with his in a casual greeting. Her stepmother's eyebrows lifted in interest, watching them. For a moment, Shandra stopped wiping her eyes.

Daria forgot that the kiss was simply playacting. There was nothing casual about her pounding heart or racing pulse. Nothing casual about how she wished Ryker would wrap his arms around her and hold her for a few minutes. However, she kept her thoughts secret and her demeanor casual.

"We're almost done here," Daria told him, hoping Shandra would take the hint.

As if on cue, Shandra released more tears. "No. We can't be done."

Ryker angled his back against a wall with a view of both women's faces. Yet he stood close to Daria as if silently telling Shandra that he'd back Daria—no matter what. Normally, Daria wouldn't have needed the support, but she felt a bit out of her element here. Shandra had never come to her about family problems before.

"Do you want me to talk to Dad?" Daria asked Shandra, knowing that the phone call would be unpleasant and ineffectual. Her father didn't take kindly to her asking about his business although he never hesitated to question her about whatever he liked.

Shandra wrapped the hankie around her index finger, then slowly tugged it loose. "Talking to that man is useless."

"Then what exactly do you want me to do?"

"Could you make me a loan?"

A loan? For what? Shandra had been wealthy in her own right before she'd married Rudolf. Why would the woman need money from Daria?

Before Daria could figure out how to respond, Ryker leaned forward, entering their conversation. "How much money would you require?"

"A few hundred thousand?"

"And how would you repay the funds?" Ryker asked.

Shandra's eyes filled with tears. "That's not your concern."

"Maybe you've forgotten that I'm Daria's new accountant and business consultant."

"This is *family* business," Shandra insisted.

"True, but if Daria wants to make a loan, the funds would come from the corporation." What he'd just said wasn't true. Daria had plenty of personal funds, but she remained silent, sensing that Ryker had spoken the lie in order to seek information. "That means it's my job to protect the company's assets. Do you have collateral?"

"I turned over my money to Rudy to manage a long time ago. But you can have my jewelry. I'll have fakes made. Rudy won't ever know."

That Shandra would go to such lengths to deceive her father took Daria aback. She'd never thought the woman sneaky.

"We aren't in the jewelry business," Ryker suggested. "Perhaps you should go to an expert?"

"There's no time."

"Why not?" Daria's alarm made her throat tight. She just wanted to write the check and get Shandra out of her office. She didn't like prying, didn't want this peek into her father's and Shandra's personal lives.

"If we don't maintain appearances then our friends will talk. The financial experts will get wind of the trouble and Harrington stock will fall. And that's why I can't go to a jeweler."

"Rudolf sent you here, didn't he?" Ryker guessed.

At his accusation, Shandra wept copiously. "I told him I couldn't pull this off."

Ryker's shrewd guess shocked Daria. After she heard Shandra's admission, she wished she knew more about the family business, but she'd been so caught up in her own problems, she'd not been aware of any financial setbacks. Her father must be desperate to send Shandra to her like this.

Without further hesitation, Daria stood and removed her purse from the hook behind her office door. Quickly, she wrote out a check and gave it to Shandra. "Let me know if you need more."

"Thank you. Thank you." Shandra carefully placed the check in her purse. "I've one more favor to ask of you."

"Yes?"

"Could you please not mention this to Rudy? He's so proud. You know how he is…"

Daria knew all too well that her father must have

hated asking his daughter for money—even secretly through an intermediary. "We'll keep this between us."

The moment Shandra left, Ryker hugged her as if he knew how badly the conversation had shaken Daria. She accepted the comfort he gave, telling herself she was simply playing her part, but not really believing it. She needed comfort, and going to him, letting him put his arms around her seemed natural.

"I've always thought of my father as invincible."

She supposed he would tell her that she'd just thrown away her money, but instead he tucked her head under his chin. "You have a generous heart."

His arms around her made her feel safe and secure, calming her nerves. She breathed in the spice of his aftershave and snuggled closer. Leaning against his chest, she wished she could leave all her problems behind and run away somewhere. Run away like Fallon? The thought startled her. Always before, Daria had sought safety in her home. She had always found comfort there by fixing herself a hot cup of tea, petting her cats and pruning her plants. The concept of leaving her home to run away with Ryker was simply a measure of how far off kilter she'd gone due to stress.

Daria could have stayed in his embrace for the rest of the day, but her secretary buzzed. "There's a call from the warehouse in Brazil. There's been a disaster."

Chapter Six

Daria put the call on speakerphone, her expression resigned. "Yes, Carlos?"

"There's been a fire." The man's Hispanic accent was thick, his tone sorrowful. "*Señorita,* you first want the good or the bad news?"

"Just tell me." Daria braced, stiffening her back.

Moments ago she'd felt soft and cuddly in his arms. Now Ryker could see the steel in her spine, the flash of anger in her eyes that portrayed a woman who had built an empire and who protected and defended what was hers. Her attitude clearly said that she would overcome whatever difficulty came her way.

Still, she didn't deserve more bad news on top of her other problems, and Ryker wondered if the fire was deliberate or accidental. He knew a professional could start an electrical fire that wouldn't appear suspicious, so they might not ever get an answer unless the police caught the culprit.

"The entire warehouse is gone."

Daria's expression didn't change but her hazel eyes darkened. "Was anyone hurt?"

"No, *señorita.*"

"The Passion Perfect seeds?"

"Safe."

Daria let out a sigh of relief. "Plant seedlings as soon as we set up another facility."

"*Sí, señorita,* but the insurance company may, how do you *Americanos* say, drag its feet."

"Why?"

"They believe someone from Harrington Bouquet may have set the fire. But my men would never do such a horrible thing. Why would they ruin their livelihood?"

For money. Ryker kept the thought to himself.

Daria picked up a pen and made notes. "Why would they think *we* started the fire?"

"The fire, it started with petrol."

Gasoline? So the arsonist hadn't even bothered to try and make the fire appear accidental. Someone was trying to make Daria's life difficult, attacking her on several fronts. But why?

Daria didn't hesitate. "Get the paperwork started. I'll ship out another greenhouse, and we'll wait on the insurance money."

"*Sì, señorita.* I am sorry."

"Just get us up and running as soon as possible. And hire guards for the day and night shifts, too."

Daria buzzed her secretary without saying a word to Ryker. "Jeanie, I'd like you to set up a press conference at two o'clock. But first send out e-mails to every store. The price of Passion Perfect flowers just went up thirty percent. Run a sale on Pink Snowflakes and Thunderclouds."

"Got it. Anything else?"

"Yes, have Isabelle purchase another greenhouse and ship it to Brazil as soon as possible."

"Okay."

"And I want round-the-clock security on every greenhouse we own."

"That's going to be expensive."

"I don't care. Do it."

Ryker waited until Daria had finished talking with her secretary and turned off the speakerphone before mildly asking, "You sure calling a press conference is a good idea?"

Daria leaned back in her chair. "If I give the press the story, I can try to put my own spin on it. If they dig up the news themselves, they might conclude that I'm going broke, or that I set the fire to collect on the insurance."

"Or that you're about to raise all the money you can before you flee and the police arrest you?"

"Exactly."

"Who has the most to gain from that fire?"

"My competitors. And the greenhouse company will now make a huge unexpected sale."

"But your competitors can't sell Passion Perfect flowers, can they?"

"No. But *we* won't have enough to go around— even with the price increase. So my customers might go elsewhere."

"You grow those flowers in other greenhouses, don't you?"

"Yes. But the demand is so high we were barely keeping up with it. Now some customers will be disappointed. Brazil was our main source."

"Can you think of anyone else who would have anything to gain by this fire?"

She frowned at him. "I'm not sure what you mean."

"Could Harry's and your sister's murders be connected in any way to the fire?"

"How?"

"That's what I'm asking you. Did Harry and Fallon ever visit the greenhouse in Brazil?"

"As a matter of fact, they were there a few weeks ago. Why?"

"I don't know." Ryker needed more pieces of the puzzle to make good connections. "What about your other employees? Have any of them been to Brazil recently?"

"Cindy, she's in charge of customer service and floral design, flew down there on vacation last month with Jeanie. But what would they have to gain by hiring someone to set a fire?"

"Probably nothing." Ryker's fingers itched for his computer keyboard. He had hours of research to complete. He needed bank, credit card and phone records of all her employees. He also needed to check out her family and her father's company.

While Harrington Industries was traded on the New York Stock Exchange and had to produce regular financial statements, after the Enron disaster, who could trust the auditors whose livelihood sometimes depended on cooking the books?

"Mike Brannigan's on line two," Jeanie's voice interrupted his thoughts.

"Now what?" Daria put him on speakerphone. "I'm busy, Mike."

"I'm hearing rumors about your company." Mike Brannigan's smooth voice invaded her office. "If you accept my offer today, I won't lower—"

"What kind of rumors?" Daria asked.

"That you have internal problems."

Could Mike Brannigan be applying pressure to try and force Daria to sell? Could he have framed her for murder and started that fire just to get his hands on her company?

"Nothing's changed, Mike. *I'll* call *you* if I change my mind."

Her business under control, Daria checked her watch, then looked at Ryker. "If we hurry, we have just enough time for lunch before the press conference."

WITH HER CAR parked so close by, Ryker didn't expect Daria to flag a taxi. "You aren't driving?"

"Not where we're going."

He understood a moment later when she instructed the driver to take them to a part of the city known for stripping a car of tires, wheels and engines in less than twenty minutes. Later, at the sight of several drug deals going down on the corner and prostitutes openly plying their trade, Ryker was glad he'd come armed.

They exited the cab and he walked beside Daria toward a building with a sign that said Big Brothers and Big Sisters. This building should have been condemned twenty years ago. The paint had faded to a muddy brown, but the brick flooring had endured through the decades. Inside, the two-story ceiling sported cracked and peeling crown molding, and what had once been an elegant chandelier now housed five bare bulbs that cast a dim light on the interior, which would have been gloomy except for the spirited activity inside.

Kids of all shapes, colors and sizes careened through the massive foyer with enthusiasm. A stereo blared out hip-hop and a group of teens weaved, slid and bobbed to the beat. In another area little kids sipped through straws stuck into cartons of milk.

From out of the group of kids by a Ping-Pong table, a thin girl emerged. A mixture of exotic cultures and races, her light brown skin and Oriental eyes lighted happily on Daria before giving Ryker the once-over.

"Ready for lunch?" Daria asked, handing her a spray of violets.

"Yeah." The child lifted the flowers to her nose and breathed in deeply. "Thanks."

"You're welcome." Daria hugged the girl, then stepped back. "Tanya Johnson, meet Ryker Stevens."

Tanya gave him a high five but her eyes appeared wary, skipping over him and never settling anywhere. "You ain't—"

"Aren't," Daria corrected.

"You aren't going to have no—"

"Any."

"You *aren't* going to have *any* time for me, right?"

Ryker watched the girl fidget under Daria's corrections. Her grammar might need some fine-tuning, but her instincts were honed to perfection. The child might not have had the advantages of a first-class education, she might have ADHD, but intelligence shined from her eyes. And someday she would be a knockout. Her nose was straight, her lips already full, and her eyes revealed the soul of a woman three times her age.

Daria placed an arm over her shoulders, and they all walked out of the building. "Why would you say that?"

"Now that you've got yourself a fine man, you won't have time for me. You'll have your own kids…"

Daria laughed. "Whoa, Tanya. Ryker's my business consultant."

"You never brought no—any," Tanya corrected herself, "business consultant to our lunches before."

Ryker wondered where they were headed. From the looks passersby were shooting their way, he estimated it wouldn't be long before they could become targets. With their expensive clothes, they stood out like tomatoes in a bin of lemons—prime for the picking. As several tattooed Hispanic brothers approached, Ryker moved closer to the women and unbuttoned his coat to gain easier access to his weapon.

And for the first time, he inserted himself into the conversation. "I'm with Daria to help her over the problems she's having right now. You've heard that the police consider her a suspect in her sister's murder?"

"Yeah, that sucks."

Ryker watched Tanya's face carefully but saw no

sign of duplicity. However, she didn't look surprised by the news, either. Although he had to consider everyone with the means and opportunity to poison the coffee as a suspect, this child had no reason to wish harm on Daria. From the look of excitement in Tanya's eyes, which she'd tried hard to hide, the girl looked forward to her weekly outings with her Big Sister.

Daria gave him one of her let-me-handle-this looks. "We're not here to talk about me. How're you doing? Still clean?"

"Yes, ma'am."

"Still having cravings?"

"For sex or drugs?"

Tanya looked about thirteen and, although Daria had mentioned that the girl had a record, the casual question shocked him. Ryker had seen girls in the Orient as young as ten selling themselves, the same in Africa, but he had not yet seen it here in the States.

Daria didn't seem the least bit shocked. She led them to a diner, and he requested a corner booth where he could sit with his back to the wall. From his position he could see everyone who approached, and while no one bothered them, he still felt as though he had a bull's-eye painted on his forehead.

"Talk," Daria ordered.

Tanya grinned, displaying a beautiful set of white teeth to go with her refined cheekbones. "I'm doing my best to avoid temptation."

Daria passed out menus. "And how's school?"

The smile evaporated. "The word going round is that you're going to get murder one."

"You know better than to believe rumors."

"Rumors often have some truth in them," Tanya countered.

Behind the bluster, Ryker saw fear in the kid's eyes. Fear for Daria or what would happen to Tanya if Daria got sent away?

"You needn't worry," Daria told Tanya. "I'm not leaving you."

"Unless they lock you up." Tanya fidgeted with the menu and bounced in her seat like a two-year-old.

Daria trembled slightly, then squared her shoulders. "If I go to jail, I'll send you money for bus fare and you can visit."

Their waitress interrupted and took their orders of burgers, fries and colas.

"Maybe you should run and hide somewhere." Tanya didn't seem happy with the prospect of visiting Daria in an upstate prison. "You ain't—aren't—staying around because of me, are you?"

Ryker knew the Big Sister program required the adults to commit to the kids for years. The organization screened applicants carefully. Children from broken homes needed stability, not more chaos in their lives.

Daria spoke firmly. "I'm staying to find Fallon and Harry's killer and to prove my innocence."

Ryker wondered whether the girl's curiosity stemmed from genuine affection for Daria or whether she would simply miss the lunch out once a week? Daria had told him she'd hoped Tanya would some-day work for her full-time. To him the kid seemed the unlikeliest of murder suspects. But she knew about poisons and she'd worked summers in the store, so she knew the operation.

Tanya sipped the cola the waitress left. "I heard the computer disappeared from the police evidence room. Will that help?"

"How'd you hear?" Ryker asked, more than startled that Tanya knew inside information that had yet to be released to the papers. The kid might be young, but she was obviously streetwise.

"One of my girlfriends sleeps with a cop."

"Does the cop have a name?" he asked.

Tanya looked at him warily. "Don't know any names." Then she turned to Daria. "The missing computer is good for you, right?"

"I don't know. Someone planted evidence against me on the computer. Without the hard drive, we can't trace who did it."

Not unless Logan Kincaid obtained a search warrant or the Internet service provider cooperated. Ryker kept those thoughts to himself. If he had to hack in, he'd rather keep the information quiet. Hacking was illegal, but if he did no damage, even if he got caught, the law would probably look the other way.

"But now the cops can't use the evidence against you, right?" Tanya insisted.

Daria nodded and then glanced at Ryker. "If Tanya doesn't accept my offer to come work full-time for Harrington Bouquet, she's going to be a fine lawyer someday."

"First I've got to get through the ninth grade," Tanya teased and then the light in her eyes dimmed

as she toyed with the flowers Daria had given her.
"I'm worried about you."

DARIA HAD TO cut their lunch short due to the sched-
uled press conference and she wasn't sure her efforts
to reassure Tanya had done much good. The girl was
too smart to believe her when the television news
channels were full of accusations against Daria.

As usual, Daria had trouble finding a taxi back to
the office and Ryker had to phone a cab company.

Beside her in the back seat of the cab, Ryker didn't
say a word. She had no idea what he thought about
her friendship with Tanya, but she hadn't liked him
questioning the girl. But then she didn't like him sus-
pecting the people who worked in her office or her
family and her friends either. There seemed no real
way to eliminate anyone as a suspect—not when anyone who'd had access to her office could have ground
up the flowers and placed them in the coffee at any
time. No one could have an alibi that covered their
every moment for weeks on end. But she'd feel better
if Ryker could narrow down the list of suspects so
she didn't feel so isolated.

He'd been on the case less than twenty-four hours,
she reminded herself. The police had spent weeks investigating, and she had yet to be arrested. She tried
to take comfort in that fact and discovered the pressure inside her had eased a little just by knowing Ryker would do whatever he could to help her. She had
no doubts about his investigative skills or his com-
petence, and he'd cut down on his "boyfriend act"
in the taxi, giving her a chance to think and regroup.

The man could turn his charm on and off like a light switch. But when he was in the "on" mode, she often responded as if his interest in her was for real. She didn't want to react. With all her problems, this was not the time for a masculine diversion. She needed all of her thoughts to be focused on her business and finding justice for her sister and Harry. And yet, during her conversations with first Shandra and then Tanya, how many times had she wondered what Ryker was thinking? How many times had she glanced his way to check his reaction?

The cab pulled up to the curb, and Ryker paid the driver. Daria had intended to head up to her office, but the crush of shoppers in the boutique caught her eye. What was up? Business was rarely this good. Had the sales of Pink Snowflakes and Thunderclouds spiked customer interest?

"I'd like to check on the store for a few minutes before going upstairs," she told Ryker.

He glanced past the signature revolving gold and black doors with etched Passion Perfect flowers in the glass to the crowd inside. "Is anything wrong?"

"I don't think so. I'm hoping the sale has pulled in more customers."

Ryker slipped his hand into hers. "Okay."

"Daria!"

Recognizing the voice that had just called her name, she almost groaned aloud. Instead, she turned on the sidewalk, keeping her hand in Ryker's, then plastered a pleasant expression on her face.

Mike Brannigan, wearing a spiffy black suit, black shirt and black tie and carrying a bulging briefcase, hurried toward her, his long legs eating up the distance within seconds. "I was hoping to catch you before the press conference."

With Mike's appearance, Ryker released Daria's hand and placed a possessive arm around her waist, drawing her against his side in a clear show of proprietary possession. She didn't appreciate the gesture. Standing close enough to breathe in his scent and feeling the hard muscles of his chest against her side distracted her. But while she needed her wits about her to deal with a sharp businessman like Mike, she also understood the necessity of consistently keeping up pretenses.

She introduced the two men, who eyed one another like prizefighters sizing up their opponents. Despite the civilized handshake, the aura surrounding the three of them simmered with hostility.

Daria looked at Mike, whose blond-haired, blue-eyed surfer looks drew women like a magnet. Then checked her watch. "I don't have long."

Mike ignored Ryker, went into his smooth-pitched sales mode and turned on his charisma. "The rumors were true. I heard about your South American fire—"

"How?" Ryker challenged.

"We buy rhodonite from Brazil."

"Rhodonite?" Daria asked.

"A reddish-pink stone that our jewelers polish into beads."

"And exactly what do your pink beads have to do with a fire?" Ryker prodded.

"I e-mail our suppliers daily. And my Brazilian

contact happened to mention the warehouse fire. I heard all the Passion Perfects went up in flames."

"Not all of them. We have others in different warehouses." She didn't mention how short her supply had become. Daria shot a glance into the shop. Milling customers inside didn't appear to be taken care of. She'd have to tell Elizabeth to hire more help. Customers didn't like waiting.

"So what's up?" she asked Mike, impatient to be on her way.

"I was hoping after your emergency—"

"A setback," she corrected him.

"That after your setback, you might change your mind and agree to announce the sale of Harrington Bouquet to me during the press conference."

He knew about the fire. He knew about the press conference. And in turn she felt as though her life was disintegrating. And like a vulture, he was there to feed off her carcass. *Stop it.* The man had his ears to the ground, that's all, but she wanted him to stay away from her business.

Despite her annoyance, Daria kept her voice level. "I don't think so, Mike, but thanks anyway."

Mike looked right, then left, then grabbed her arm, losing his salesman mode and sounding desperate. "You need to sell to me soon."

Ryker's eyes narrowed. "What's the rush?"

"This is between me and Daria."

Ryker spoke in a velvet tone laced with steel. "As far as I'm concerned, there's nothing between you and Daria—unless *she* tells me otherwise."

Mike ignored Ryker and clung to her arm. "You could lose everything if you don't sell now."

"What are you talking about?" Daria asked. Mike might be persistent, but he wasn't prone to dramatics. In spite of herself she had to tamp down a spike of alarm.

"A takeover."

"We're not a public corporation."

"But your bank can call in the loan."

"My payments are up-to-date."

"They'll use the morals clause to get rid of you."

Ryker shifted his stance and casually broke Mike's hold on her arm. "What's a morals clause?"

"If Daria is deemed unfit to run the company, her bankers can call in the loan."

"That's if I'm senile or insane," she said.

Ryker frowned. "This doesn't sound like a real threat. Can't your lawyers tie up the bank in court for years?"

"Probably not. Banks write the loans in their favor. If they recall the loan and I don't pay, they can foreclose."

She could lose everything she and Fallon had worked so hard to attain. And now without her sister, she felt more responsible than ever for carrying on her legacy.

Daria flinched at the police siren blaring a few blocks away. Ever since her sister's death, she hadn't been able to think of the police as protective. While they weren't the enemy, she remained on edge around uniformed officers and detectives alike.

Mike's face tightened with intensity. "The bankers

will argue that someone who murdered her sister is insane, unqualified to run the company, too great a risk for the bank to take.''

Daria wasn't concerned and steeled herself not to flinch again as the sirens grew louder. ''So I'll get another loan.''

''Once one bank drops you, the others will back off a deal. You know that.''

''And why are *you* so concerned?'' Ryker took Daria's hand. ''Seems to me, that would be the perfect time for you to swoop in and get a bargain price.''

Mike scowled at Ryker. ''I'd rather pay more for a company with an unsullied reputation. If Daria drags the name through the dirt, Harrington Bouquet is of no use to me. And I'd like Daria to get a good price. We *are* friends.''

The police car pulled up to the curb with a screech. Reporters converged on the sidewalk. At the same time, a customer burst out the doors of the shop and ran up to the uniformed officers.

A customer pointed back at Harrington Bouquet. ''The store manager's dead. She was fine, then ate a piece of candy, gagged and dropped to the floor. She was poisoned. Just like those other people.''

Chapter Seven

Ryker took one look at Daria's white face and grabbed her. She'd held up well during the morning's crisis, but to face Elizabeth's death so soon after her sister's and brother-in-law's had undoubtedly brought back the entire horrible tragedy. He feared she might faint and expected her to lean on him. Instead, with frantic strength, she broke free of his grip and raced across the wide but crowded sidewalk toward the store, making surprisingly fast time in her heels, leaving Ryker and Mike behind.

Ryker took off after her. When she almost knocked over a uniformed cop in her haste, Ryker caught up with her. Daria's eyes looked wild enough to beat the officer with her fists, but her control hadn't abandoned her. She straightened her back, ignored the flashing bulbs of the press.

She faced the cop. "I'm the president of this company. Let me through."

The reporters she'd called in for the press conference were getting more than they bargained for. So convenient. As if the murder had been staged to take advantage of Daria's situation, which once again led him to believe an insider had set her up.

But now was no time for solving the mystery. Daria might be strong and holding herself together for the moment, but he suspected that she was hanging on to her control by the narrowest of margins.

Reporters thrust microphones in her face. "Did the poison come from Passion Perfect flowers again?"

"Did you brew Elizabeth's coffee and hand it to her?"

"Are your father's connections in city hall keeping you out of jail, Ms. Harrington?"

"How do you feel about your manager's death?"

Ryker stifled a curse. How did they expect her to feel? *Bastards.*

Ryker helped Daria shove past the reporters, knowing she needed to go to her friend's side, yet wanting to protect her from the sight of the body. Death by poisoning wasn't clean or pretty. Often the muscles contracted into a grotesque death mask that captured the victim's last agonizing and terrified moments. He wished he could spare Daria more pain, but knew he couldn't.

Daria hadn't believed in running away from the previous murders, and she wouldn't go easy on herself by avoiding the ugly scene now. If he held her back, she'd resent his interference, but he wanted her to know she wasn't alone.

He took her cold hand in his, whispered in her ear, "You'll get through this."

She didn't respond except to squeeze his hand more

tightly. At least she recognized his presence, knew he was there for her.

Due to his height, he could already see the body's feet sticking out from the edge of the front counter. Homicide detectives had arrived, roped off the crime scene but kept the customers nearby and were conducting interviews. He tucked Daria under his arm, hoping she wouldn't ever see the body.

A homicide detective met them inside the door. Young, sharp-eyed and low-key, he led them away from the body back toward the front of the store. Briefly Ryker wondered why he hadn't taken them into the private passage that led to Daria's office. Maybe he was inexperienced. The detective's red hair, green eyes and fresh-scrubbed face gave him a boyish appearance, yet he carried himself with the demeanor of a man who knew his business.

Daria's voice shook but she kept her chin high. "Detective O'Brien. What happened?"

Obviously she knew the man. Likely the same detective had questioned her about her sister''s and Harry's deaths.

"Elizabeth Hinze was your store manager?"

"And friend."

"By my best estimate she died twenty minutes ago," he told her.

Although she trembled, Daria looked him straight in the eye. "Was she poisoned like the reporters said?"

"We won't know until the tox screen comes back in a few weeks."

"Your best guess, Detective?" Ryker asked.

O'Brien turned his sharp-eyed attention on Ryker and gave him the thorough once-over that cops did so well. "And you are?"

"Harrington Bouquet's—" Ryker put his arm around Daria "—newest employee." With his free hand, he slowly pulled out a card from an inside pocket of his jacket. "You can verify my background by calling this number."

The business card had a CIA logo. While technically, Ryker had never worked directly for the Agency, the Shey Group's close ties to the organization was the fastest way for him to gain the officer's trust. And he badly wanted that trust, as well as an inside source. Only then could he help influence the police to look for another suspect besides Daria.

One step at a time.

O'Brien glanced at the logo, then again looked hard at Ryker. "You can be sure I'll do a thorough check."

"I'm willing to cooperate. Would it help Miss Harrington's case for you to know that she hasn't been out of my sight for the past twenty hours?"

"No, it wouldn't."

At the cop's words, Daria sagged against Ryker, just a little. She was too smart not to know she'd just become the suspect in her friend's murder, too.

O'Brien consulted his notes. "Another clerk told me that Elizabeth had been hoarding her chocolate since her birthday four weeks ago. The poison could have been placed inside the chocolate truffles at any time."

"So it *was* poison?" Ryker asked.

"Looks like it."

Daria straightened. "The poison that killed my sister was from Passion Perfect flower petals ground in with the beans. How could the petals be put on chocolate without Elizabeth noticing?"

The detective consulted his notes again, but Ryker suspected he already knew those facts and was simply using the extra bit of time to decide exactly how much to reveal. "I'm told the poison is tasteless and odorless."

"It is," Daria agreed. "But Elizabeth knew what to look for. She should have seen the—"

"Not if someone mixed the poison into a solution and shot it inside the chocolate's center with a hypodermic needle," Ryker told her.

"That's possible?" Daria's eyes widened. "But why? Why would anyone want to kill Elizabeth?"

"When was the last time you saw her alive?" Detective O'Brien asked.

"This morning when we left for lunch, I saw her in the store through the window," Daria told him.

"And the last time you were face-to-face?"

"Yesterday in my office."

An ambulance with sirens screaming pulled up to the curb.

"Any trouble between you?"

Daria shook her head.

"Was she having problems with anyone? Family? An old lover?"

"Not that I know of."

"Did she have a boyfriend?"

Daria hesitated.

The detective's pen paused over his notepad. "Answer the question, please, Ms. Harrington."

"I saw her kissing a man but I'm not sure if it was a onetime thing."

"I thought you were friends." O'Brien looked up from his notes. "Wouldn't your friend have shared?"

"Normally, we did."

"But?" O'Brien pressed.

Ryker saw no reason to shield Daria's brother from the police. "Last night, we came by the store and Elizabeth was there with Peter Harrington. They were kissing."

"I don't think Elizabeth and Peter wanted me to know about their relationship," Daria added.

"Why?" O'Brien asked.

"Maybe they thought I wouldn't approve. Many women go after Peter for his wealth and position. And Elizabeth had so little in the way of material possessions that maybe she'd assume I'd group her in with the others. But she would never date a man just because he had money."

"You sure of that?" the detective asked.

"Elizabeth worked her way up from nothing. She was the first person in her family to graduate from college. Someday, she wanted to open her own floral shop."

"Maybe she saw your brother as a shortcut and you as an obstacle."

"But she's the one who's dead," Daria protested.

"Yeah, maybe you didn't like Elizabeth dating little brother," O'Brien suggested.

Daria gasped, then tightened her lips and remained silent.

"There's one hole in your theory, Detective." Ryker kept a firm hold of Daria. "Daria only learned about Peter and Elizabeth's relationship yesterday. Since that time, Daria has spent every moment with either me, her secretary or her stepmother."

"Maybe she knew they were an item before yesterday and only pretended surprise," O'Brien countered.

Ryker had no answer for the cop. And a commotion in the private entrance caught his eye. The emergency medical people had entered there. The door opened and they carried Peter Harrington out on a stretcher.

His face was twisted in pain. Grayish. And he was moaning, his hand clutched to his gut.

Daria screamed, ran forward and shoved people out of the way to get to her brother's side. "Oh my God. What happened?"

"Poison," he whispered.

Then someone covered his mouth and nose with an oxygen mask and others carried him away.

Ryker's thoughts raced. The detective had known all along about Peter. That's why he'd avoided taking them to the hallway earlier. No doubt O'Brien had been hoping that Daria would say something to incriminate herself.

Daria followed the stretcher out onto the sidewalk. She ignored the press and flashbulbs. Quietly she spoke to one of the emergency workers. "My brother, is he going to live?"

"Ma'am, they can give you that information at the hospital."

THE AMBULANCE TOOK Peter straight to the emergency room. After Daria and Ryker arrived at the hospital, she learned, much to her frustration, that she wasn't allowed to accompany the patient into the emergency room.

She didn't make a fuss about going to Peter's side, knowing her father would do so when he arrived. Wanting to wait for news before telling him what had happened to his favorite child, but unable to deny her father a chance to be with his son in a time of need, Daria phoned her parents.

"What do you mean he's been poisoned?" Rudy roared through the receiver. "I'll be there in twenty minutes." He clicked off the phone in Daria's ear. She winced, but had expected no less. After a quick call to Isabelle, placing her in charge of Harrington Bouquet's day-to-day operations, Daria sank into a chair in the corner of the waiting room, shocked, angry and scared.

A TV buzzed in the background. Sick people waited for medical attention, worried persons for news of their loved ones. They sat leafing through ragged magazines or got up and went outside to smoke.

Daria ignored their pain. She was too full of her own grief and anger to feel for others. How could this be happening to her family again?

Ryker thrust a bottle of water into her hand, and she twisted off the cap and drank, all the while thinking a shot of liquor might have been more appropriate. Still, she appreciated the gesture. Her mouth and throat were so dry that she was having difficulty swallowing. She downed half the bottle in a few gulps.

"Thanks."

"I coaxed one of the nurses into giving me information. Apparently, Peter only took a bite of the chocolate and immediately vomited. They're pumping his stomach now. They think they got to him in time."

"Thank God."

"Who gave Elizabeth her birthday chocolate?"

"I did."

Daria still couldn't believe Elizabeth was gone. Damn. Damn. Damn. She'd worked so hard to improve her lot in life. And now she was dead.

"Who else knew that you gave her the chocolate?"

"Everyone in the office. We had a party."

Daria would never again come home after a hard day of work to find her friend fussing with the plants. Never again share their late-night girl talks that sometimes lasted until dawn. Never again see her smiling face behind the counter of the Fifth Avenue store again.

And Peter, the golden child. Happy-go-lucky Peter with the ever-ready smile and warm hugs—she couldn't bear to think of losing him, too.

As a kid, on the rare occasions when the sisters had been home, Peter had tagged after them like a little pest. He'd been their parents' favorite, the spoiled baby who'd gotten all their love, and yet she and Fallon could never hold that against him. He was too

sweet and adorable. Her brother had never complained when his father started grooming him to take
on the huge responsibility of running the Harrington
conglomerate.

While brother and sisters hadn't been close due to
their eight-year age difference, Peter had often de-
flected his parents' wrath from her and Fallon's shoulders. He never failed to speak up for them—and now
he was lying in that hospital room, maybe dying due
to the same poison that had taken Fallon and Elizabeth from her. No way could she return to work until
she knew for certain that he would live.

During the time Daria had spent mourning her sister, Isabelle had taken over running the stores and she
would take care of the company during the current
crisis, but the older woman didn't like the responsibility. Daria reminded herself that whatever happened
she couldn't leave Isabelle in charge for too long
without overburdening the woman, who was getting
on in years.

"So everyone had access to the chocolates?" Ryker asked.

Daria nodded. "Elizabeth had to watch her weight
like me, but she always loved to get candy for her
birthday. She liked every kind of chocolate, the
creams, nuts, caramels, peanut butter and even pep-
permints. We never could find one that Elizabeth
didn't like." Leaning over, Daria rested her elbows
on her knees and placed her face in her hands.

Ryker rubbed the back of her neck, his strong fingers kneading muscles knotted with tension. She
knew he was trying to comfort her but she couldn't

accept, didn't deserve, comfort—not when her brother could be dying. "If Peter doesn't make it…"

"He will," he told her again. "He's young and strong and a fighter. He's going to pull through."

"But if he doesn't…"

"Daria."

Eyeballs gritty and dry, she lifted her head. "What?"

"The press is going to accuse you of attempting to murder both of your siblings—even if Peter lives."

It wasn't fair. Daria had no reason to kill Elizabeth—even if she'd known her friend was dating her brother and hadn't approved, that wasn't a motive for murder.

Ryker had told her what he believed the press would print. His voice had been gentle, and she knew he'd only spoken the harsh words to prepare her for what was ahead. But the statement felt like a direct blow to her heart. She had to force air into her lungs. Breathing was an effort, tiring her more than she'd have thought possible. Once again in her mind's eye she relived Fallon's and Harry's horrible deaths. The surprise, the paralysis, the death masks of terror.

Oh, God. She wasn't yet ready to face her family, never mind the outside world, the press and the cops.

Just let Peter live, she prayed. Let him make a full recovery. The thought of him lying in that bed, mindless or paralyzed, was more than she could bear. She started to tremble, then shake.

"Hey, hey. I'm sorry." Ryker pulled her to her feet and into his arms. "Think positive thoughts."

"I can't."

"You can."

"But what if—"

"Shh." He tipped up her chin, looked into her eyes. "This wasn't your fault."

"It could have been."

"How?"

"If someone's trying to hurt me by—"

"Then it's their fault. Not yours."

"So why do I feel responsible?" she countered.

"Because that's what you do in a crisis. You take everything onto your shoulders. Solve the problem. Fix what is broken. Forge ahead. Only this time, control of the situation is out of your hands."

Just then, her father and Shandra barged through the front door of the hospital like a whirlwind. Shandra was dressed to the nines in her designer dress, her father in an immaculate suit and tie. True to form, her father started making demands.

Arms flailing in huge gestures, Rudolf raised his voice before he even reached the information desk. "I donated a wing to this hospital. I expect my son to receive the very best of care. The best. A specialist. I won't have an intern touching him. I want the chief of surgery—"

The woman behind the front desk responded kindly. "Sir, your son doesn't require surgery."

"You aren't listening," Rudolf sputtered. "I want to talk to his doctor right now. You hear me? Right now."

"Dad." Daria broke from Ryker's embrace and hurried toward her father. "Please. You'll give yourself a heart attack."

Shandra shouted shrilly at Daria. "You'd like that, wouldn't you! Then all you'd have to do is kill me next, and you'd inherit everything this family owns."

Shandra had made so much noise that reporters outside could hear every word. Daria didn't deserve her savage verbal attack. Not that she'd expected to buy her stepmother's love with the large check she'd written, but she hadn't expected such viciousness.

Daria sensed Ryker was ready to defend her, but she'd had plenty of practice in that department. "Shandra, if you don't lower your voice, I'll knock your teeth down your throat and give those reporters pictures to go along with their stories."

Rudolf reached out to grab Daria's shoulder. "How dare you—"

Ryker somehow planted himself between her and her father's grasping fingers. "Sir. Why don't we all sit down and talk where the press can't overhear every word?"

"Rudy!" Shandra burst into tears. "Are you going to let your daughter, that murderer, talk to me like that?"

"I want to know what's going on," Rudolf spoke more calmly.

Stomach churning at the ugly scene, Daria allowed Ryker to lead her back to the relatively private corner of the waiting room where they had been sitting earlier, leaving her father and Shandra to follow or not as they liked.

They followed. Rudolf sat down so hard, the chair skidded back several inches. "What happened?"

"Yes, tell us." Shandra removed a hankie from her

purse and spread it over the chair before sitting, as if fearing contamination.

Their rude outburst might be over, but Daria wouldn't forget the hostile words. How could she, when Shandra had called her a murderer? But she put the hurt aside and fought back her nausea to give her father some hope.

"We don't know much more than I told you on the phone," Daria began. Then, numb and cold, she repeated to her parents what the nurse had told Ryker.

"How long before we can see Peter?" her father demanded.

"After they move him to a private room, I'd imagine," Daria speculated.

A doctor wearing blue scrubs strode through the double doors into the waiting room and approached their corner. "You are the Harrington family? I'm Dr. Sidholm."

"How's my son?" Rudolf demanded.

"Peter will make a complete recovery. We're going to keep him overnight for observation. If everything goes as well as we expect, we can release him tomorrow."

"Thank God!" Shandra started crying again, this time from relief and joy.

"When can we see him?" Rudolf asked in a more pleasant tone.

Dr. Sidholm frowned. "I suppose you'll have to ask the guards stationed by his door."

"Guards?" Daria asked. Surely the murderer wouldn't try again.

"A Detective O'Brien is with Peter now. He'll be

able to answer your questions better than I can. Now, if you'll excuse me, I have other patients."

Her parents turned away, rushing toward the elevators without another word.

"Doctor," Daria said. "Thank you for all that you've done."

"You're welcome. Your brother seems like a fine young man. He never once asked about himself. All his concern was for a girl named Elizabeth."

"She didn't make it," Ryker spoke softly.

"I'm sorry." Dr. Sidholm left them with a shake of her head.

Daria walked toward the elevators with Ryker, emotions of relief at her brother's expected recovery battling with grief over Elizabeth's death. She realized that if Ryker hadn't been there, her parents would have rushed off anyway and left her alone.

And she was so grateful not to be alone right now. She squeezed his hand. "I know it's your job, but thanks for being here anyway."

Ryker stopped walking right in the middle of the hallway. The traffic parted, people ignoring them and hurrying by, leaving them isolated.

Ryker placed one hand on each of her shoulders as they stood toe to toe. "Let's get a few things straight."

"This isn't the time…"

His eyes narrowed on her with a fierce protectiveness. "If I waited for you to pick the moment, this conversation would never happen."

She flung her hair back in a defiant gesture. "What then? Tell me and get it over with."

"I'm not here with you right now just because of my job."

She sucked in her breath. "You aren't?"

"I'm here because I want to be here with you."

"Okay."

"I'm here because you need me."

Of course she did, that's why she'd hired him in the first place. But then she looked into the embers burning in his eyes and suddenly realized that he'd just taken their relationship to a different level. He'd meant that she'd needed him as a friend. As a man.

She wanted to deny that he was right. She didn't want to need anyone. She wanted to rely on her own ingenuity to find the killer and her own strength to get through this emergency and the pending murder charges she still faced.

If she ever had, she no longer considered him an employee. In the short time they'd been together, she'd come to rely on his good judgment, his experience and expertise. But even more, she'd come to rely on his supportive strength. She did need him.

Knowing that one person believed in her innocence gave her the courage to keep going. She hadn't wanted to admit that she needed him. But now that she had, what was she going to do about it?

Chapter Eight

Daria was still on her feet, operating on pure guts. Ryker knew that most people would have fallen apart long before now. But the only thing that Daria didn't seem to know how to deal with was honest affection. When he had stated that she needed him, she'd turned silent. She'd stared at him in astonishment and then in wonder, before she had thought to look down in an attempt to hide her feelings. But he'd seen enough. Enough to know that she was vulnerable. After what she'd already been through, she didn't need any more hurt on account of him.

He wanted to take her home, but he knew better than to suggest leaving the hospital when she wanted to see her brother. However, he dreaded taking her upstairs where her parents might turn on her again. And he feared that this time, Peter might side with them against her.

Ryker moved away from the personal conversation, which had obviously made her uncomfortable. "Peter's probably worn-out."

"I just want to see him for a minute. Give him a hug."

She didn't say the words but he understood that she needed to reassure herself that he was alive. And Ryker couldn't refuse.

They took the elevator up and spotted Peter's private room—conspicuous due to the guard outside the door. Detective O'Brien was exiting the room just as her parents entered.

"Let's give your folks a few minutes alone with Peter," Ryker suggested, then faced the detective. "Could Peter tell you anything helpful?"

"Only that Elizabeth swallowed the entire chocolate in one bite about thirty seconds before Peter bit into his. After he saw her reaction, he stuck his fingers down his throat and made himself vomit. Since he'd only ingested a tiny quantity of poison and upchucked almost immediately, he survived. His quick thinking saved his life."

"Did anyone hand them the candy?" Ryker asked.

"He says he picked the chocolates out of the box at random. We've got the remaining candy and the foil wrappers and box. Maybe we'll get lucky and pick up some prints. And we'll test every piece for poison."

Remembering that Daria's computer had been wiped clean of prints, Ryker doubted the cops would find any incriminating evidence on the candy wrappers or box. Whoever was using the poison hadn't left them any obvious clues to follow.

Poison was known as the murder weapon of women for a variety of reasons. Poisoning someone didn't take physical strength, and the killer needn't even watch her victims die. But it was also difficult to predetermine who would end up as a victim. Elizabeth could have offered a piece of candy to any employee or customer. So had this been a random murder—like those caused by poisoned aspirin or cereal in a grocery store? Or had the victim been preselected somehow?

"Detective," Daria asked, "am I the only suspect in this murder, too?"

"Right now, I can't say." O'Brien looked her directly in the eye. "But you bought Elizabeth the candy, and you have the most to gain from your brother's death, since if he'd died, you would be your parents' sole heir."

"How could I have known Elizabeth would give my brother a piece?" she asked the detective.

"Maybe you told her he had a sweet tooth."

"I didn't even know they'd be together until last night," Daria denied again.

"So you say."

"But you *are* looking at other...possibilities?" Ryker asked.

The detective glanced down the corridor, then led them away from Peter's doorway until there was no chance of anyone accidentally overhearing his words. "The D.A. is frothing to make a conviction. What does Ware have against you, Ms. Harrington?"

"Ware hates my father. A long time ago both men loved my mother."

O'Brien frowned. "Your mother?"

"She died when I was a child. Ware blames my father for her death."

"So why would Ware want to convict the daughter of the woman he loved?" O'Brien asked.

"Ware hates my father so much, it outweighs anything else."

"I see." O'Brien glanced down at the business card Ryker had given him a few hours ago. "I've checked your background, Mr. Stevens."

"Ryker."

"You get anything useful at all, I'll be happy to look into it."

"Appreciate the cooperation." The two men shook hands, then O'Brien headed to the elevator.

After the detective left, Daria glanced at Ryker, questions in her eyes. "Detective O'Brien's attitude sure changed after he looked into *your* history."

"The Shey Group has connections in high places."

"And those high places filter all the way to the New York Police Department?"

"We've done a lot of favors for law enforcement, at all levels."

"Thanks." Daria rose on her toes and kissed his cheek. "Seems like I'm always thanking you."

"That part was just doing my job."

"I'm having a little trouble keeping straight exactly what is part of your job and what isn't."

"Kissing you isn't."

He tugged her into his arms, dipped his head until their lips almost touched, giving her the opportunity to pull away if she wished.

She didn't.

Daria placed her arms around him, her fingers drawing sensuous circles on the back of his neck and shooting desire straight to his brain. As if she'd hard-wired his circuits for a kiss, without thought he brought his mouth down hard. He meant to be tender, but he couldn't hold back.

She parted her soft full lips, welcoming him with a moan of invitation. He gathered her closer, tasting her fully, his head spinning with a blend of lust and wonder at the delicious sensations.

"She's disgusting." Shandra's shrilly accented words broke through Ryker's passion. He forced himself to pull away from Daria, but not so fast that Rudolf couldn't guess what they'd been doing before he emerged to stand behind his wife in the hospital room's doorway.

Shandra's voice was loud enough to wake the terminally ill. "Peter's lying in his hospital bed and this tart of a daughter is—"

"Don't speak to her like that," Ryker warned, his temper high, his voice hard despite his lowered tone. As his anger spiked, his head cleared of passion.

"I'll speak to her any way I please, won't I, Rudy?"

"Not while I'm here, you won't." Ryker eased behind the couple into Peter's room, drawing a shaken Daria with him. Then he shut the door in her parents' faces and leaned against it, ignoring their frantic knocks to come inside.

The guard standing by Peter's bed looked more amused than concerned. He nodded at Ryker in greeting. Clearly, O'Brien had informed him of Ryker's status. But the police officer watched Daria closely, indicating that she wasn't to be trusted.

Daria didn't notice. Her eyes shining with love, she hurried to Peter and took his hand. "The doctor said you're going to be fine."

Peter, pasty white, spoke as if talking hurt his throat. "Elizabeth?"

Daria jerked. "No one told you?"

Peter shook his head.

Ryker kept his position against the door, which her parents kept trying to open. Outside, they were demanding that the guard do something.

Daria ignored the commotion and told Peter the sad news. "Elizabeth swallowed the entire piece of candy."

"But—" Peter croaked.

"She didn't make it, Peter." Daria scooted onto a corner of the bed, sat next to her brother and smoothed back his hair. "I'm sorry. I know you and Elizabeth had become good friends recently. I'll…miss her, too."

Peter turned his head away from Daria and closed his eyes, shutting her out, keeping his pain to himself. Either he wanted to grieve in private, or he'd turned away from Daria because he blamed her. Ryker wasn't sure. But Daria had a stricken look on her face that made Ryker leave his position at the door to go to her side.

He placed a hand on her shoulder. "Peter probably needs to be alone now. We should go."

Peter didn't say a word. After several moments of tense silence Daria stood, her entire body trembling.

Before Ryker could say more, her parents burst back into the room. Rudolf's face was red with anger.

Shandra had a wildness in her eyes, almost a madness that kept Ryker prepared to defend Daria if she decided to do something foolish like attack.

Shandra looked at Peter lying so still on the bed with his eyes closed and used words like a weapon. "The police should never have let you in here. What have you done to my son now?"

Daria didn't answer. She didn't look at Shandra or her father. With her head high, she let Ryker take her out of the hospital and didn't say a word during the walk to the garage where they'd left her car.

She didn't protest when he took the keys to her car from her trembling fingers and helped her into the passenger seat. He drove. She didn't ask any questions. She didn't seem to notice that he'd taken complete control of where they were going.

Ryker thought it odd that she hadn't cried. She hadn't raged. She was too quiet, keeping her emotions all balled up. Obviously she didn't want to talk. Or perhaps, she couldn't. Not yet.

So he gave her time to come to terms with everything that had happened today. He'd let her unwind at her own pace. Sometimes silence could be healing. She sure didn't need to make the extra effort to reassure him that she'd be fine. He knew she would recover. She was strong.

Ryker didn't think twice about where to take her. She would want to go home, to the soothing retreat she'd built in the middle of the steel city. So he drove straight to her penthouse, wondering all the while what he'd do if she didn't snap out of her silence. He'd come to care for Daria Harrington in a very short time. And right now he was willing to do anything to comfort her.

DARIA OPENED HER purse, but couldn't find the key to her front door. A moment of panic set in before she recalled the key now hung from a string around her neck. Her overreaction to the problem only proved how horrible her day had been.

After she finally unlocked the door, hopefully without Ryker noticing her high state of tension, she stared at the new security system in dismay. A red light blinked a thirty-second countdown. She had twenty seconds to enter her code before the system automatically alerted the police to an intruder.

And her mind went blank. "I can't remember the damn code."

"No big deal." Ryker reached over her shoulder and punched it in, then locked the door behind them.

Daria didn't know why she hated other people to see her weaknesses, but she did. Probably it went back to her childhood and having to be strong to win her father's attention. Before she understood that he ignored her simply because she was female, she'd deliberately cultivated the habit of controlling her feelings, of exhibiting strength in the face of a crisis. However, the strain of holding everything together had her on a short fuse.

Ryker had a way of soothing the raw edges of her stress. He didn't rag her about forgetting the code. He didn't force her to talk or try to distract her.

The plants inside her apartment should have calmed her. But the greenery reminded her of the loss of Elizabeth and the horror of almost losing Peter, too. She felt as though someone had taken her safe world and tossed it into a pit of garbage, throwing in evil elements that had grabbed hold and wouldn't let go. Evil that she couldn't fight. Evil that stalked her with relentless determination and that left her shivering with cold.

Daria didn't think she'd ever feel warm again. She considered taking a sauna or a hot whirlpool bath, but she felt like glass about to shatter and only the comfort of human arms would keep her world glued together. She turned around to find Ryker watching her carefully, as if he expected her to break down. And she wanted to, desperately wanted release from the emotions pummeling her.

Why was asking for his help so difficult? He couldn't read her mind. She had to force the words through her lips. "Hold me?"

She didn't have to ask twice.

He wrapped her in his arms, drawing her against his heat. She inhaled deeply, drawing his masculine scent straight into her lungs and absorbing his essence into her pores. Could he sense that leaning into his embrace made her feel less isolated? Less alone.

Ever since Fallon's death, Daria had missed her daily chats on the phone with her sister. She'd missed sharing the responsibility of the business, but most of all, she'd missed having someone to talk to, someone to whom she could speak her mind without first considering the impact of her words. Fallon had loved Daria unconditionally, loved her for her strengths and her weaknesses, her good points and her bad.

But her sister had been killed. Murdered. And the loss stayed with Daria every waking minute. And now in the span of two months, she had lost her best friend. Almost lost the brother she loved.

Somehow Daria's life had swung way out of control. She couldn't count on people she knew being alive tomorrow. She couldn't count on holding on to her business. She couldn't even count on not going to jail.

His arm around her, Ryker led her through the plants in the foyer and she spied a cat leaping for cover. "I was captured during a mission in Panama," he began.

She had no idea what he was talking about or why he'd started telling her this story out of the blue, but his words drew her out of her own depressing thoughts. She hadn't known he'd been captured.

"It wasn't the bad food or daily sessions with the T-man—"

"T-man?"

"T was short for torture. I had information that they wanted."

Daria strode beside him, leaning into the comfort of his solidity. "Why didn't you give them the information they wanted?"

"Because too many good men would have died."

Ryker had never talked about his past to her before, and she was curious about him. Besides, learning about him was so much preferable to thinking about her problems that she suspected he'd deliberately brought up the conversation to distract her. His tactic was working.

"The food inside the prison wasn't fit for man or beast. Clean water, sanitation and medical care were nonexistent. I was undercover, a kite."

"A kite?"

"It means that if you're caught, your country cuts the string and all ties. I was on my own and could expect no official help from the authorities."

She knew better than to ask about the mission. "How long were you in prison?"

"Several weeks. I missed my family."

"You've never spoken about them." Except the mother he'd lost at a young age and a father, an alcoholic.

"We're trained not to mention anything personal that can come back to hurt those we love. My father died of cirrhosis of the liver when I was twenty-two. I have an older brother, Donald, who is married and has three kids, and a younger sister, Lucy, now a lawyer in Chicago."

"Are you close?"

"We were tight as children, especially after Mom died, but later, after I joined the service, we drifted apart. But when I was in that prison, I had lots of time to think. What I regretted most—besides getting caught—was that I hadn't kept in touch. Now I see Donald and Lucy whenever I can and we talk frequently on the phone."

They strolled through her home, and she led him toward the heated tub that pulled her like a flower to the summer sun. "I keep swimsuits for guests over there." She pointed to a closet with robes and towels.

"How about sharing a whirlpool and you can finish your story?"

"Sounds good."

She hoped the change in location wouldn't alter his loquacious mood. She changed quickly and entered the tub. The water warmed her flesh, but couldn't take the chill from her bones.

She had a great view of him when he exited the bathroom. His bare chest was broad, softly dusted with curly black hair that tapered in a V down to his flat stomach. For a man who sat in front of a computer for most of the day, he had surprisingly well-formed muscles—and lots of scars.

From the T-man? She'd noted how lightly he'd skipped over that part of his story. Obviously, he'd endured much, but he had survived.

He eased into the bubbling water with a sigh, leaned back and closed his eyes.

"Don't you dare go to sleep on me."

He opened his eyes and the heat in them made her catch her breath. He wasn't sleepy. His look was hot, seductive, revealing that sleep had to be the last thing on his mind. But just as clearly, he was determined not to make the first move toward her.

"Why did you tell me about being in prison?" she asked, wondering why he'd picked that part of his history to share with her.

"I was in a cell with ten other men. Luckily I spoke Spanish, but I was the only American. We didn't ex-actly bond."

And he hadn't exactly answered her question. She suspected he was telling her the cleaned-up version and had vastly understated the horror of the conditions.

"Although none of us thought we'd ever see our families again, everyone feared that talking to me would bring down the wrath of the guards. And I figured that any of them could be a plant to get me to talk, a way to force me to break my silence."

She finally understood. "You were surrounded by people, but were alone."

"I figured that after the T-man was done with me—I wouldn't live to see another day."

She shuddered, and she moved to the seat next to him, letting her hip brush against his. At least she wasn't yet locked in a cell and she had Ryker to talk to. "It sounds like it was hopeless, but you're here."

"Harry saved me."

Harry? She looked at him in surprise. She hadn't known that the men had worked together or even known one another. "How did Harry save you?"

"He tried bribing the authorities and threatening the warden." Ryker grinned. "But when neither tactic worked, he broke me out of prison and disguised me as a nun."

At the image of Ryker in robes, Daria grinned. Especially after she'd seen his magnificent body, which matched the very male heat in his eyes. Yet, acting the perfect gentleman, he hadn't done more than hold her to comfort her.

Now he sank into the water, leaned his head back against the rim, closed his eyes and extended his arms out to both sides. With his elbows bent, his hands rested lightly on the pool's edge in a totally relaxed position.

It figured. She finally wanted him to do something and he ignored her.

Daria no longer felt like keeping herself separate and apart. She no longer wanted words of comfort or even silence. She wanted a physical connection, all that he could offer. Up until this moment, she'd thought she wanted to be held, cuddled. But now, sitting alone with Ryker in the hot whirlpool tub, remembering the power of his kiss—how his lips on hers in the hospital had ever so briefly flushed anger and fear from her thoughts, she'd changed her mind. Her life might be falling apart around her. She'd already lost Fallon, Harry and Elizabeth. Peter blamed her for his almost dying. Her father and his wife hated her more than ever. She might go to jail. Lose the business. She seemed to have no control over her destiny.

So it suddenly seemed crucial to her to take control of one part of her life. She wanted him. And she wanted to have him her way. She wanted to be in charge. Take back a measure of herself that had been lost in the last two frustrating months.

And once she made the decision to go forward, she found the wracking tension in her shoulders ease, replaced by another kind of tightness in the pit of her stomach.

She wanted to make love to this man. She wanted the intimate bond, but she didn't quite know how to go about letting him know.

Daria knew Ryker well enough to realize that he

wouldn't make a move on her—not if he thought she was vulnerable, which in so many ways she was.

So she would have to convey her change of heart. She didn't expect he would refuse her. But then why did her tummy flutter? Why did her nerves feel stretched and raw and taut? Why was her pulse roaring in her ears so loudly that she could barely think?

Daria wasn't inexperienced, just out of practice. She boldly placed her hand on Ryker's thigh. When he didn't react, didn't change expression, her heart thundered in her chest.

Ever so slowly, she ran her fingers up the outside of his leg, and down the inside, each movement light and suggestive. Beneath her palm, his corded muscles twitched. And Ryker sucked in a breath. But he didn't open his eyes and he didn't reach out to touch her.

"Please, don't move," she requested.

"Okay."

Hmm.

She considered him like a feast spread before her. Where did she want to sample first? With a nibble on his lips? A bite on the shoulder?

For the moment, she savored his long eyelashes and the arrogant line of his nose. She appreciated his sharp cheekbones offset by full lips, and his muscular neck that sloped to broad shoulders and a powerful chest that had her fingers itching to touch.

She floated from her position by his side to face him head-on, and decided that although he might be attractive as a sculpture, she wanted to disturb his equilibrium the same way he did hers.

Gently, she parted his thighs and kneeled on the

seat between his legs. He didn't resist, didn't open his eyes, but the quick beat of the pulse in his neck told her that he was very aware of her presence.

Placing her fingertips on his temples, she skimmed her fingers down his cheeks, explored his ears and dipped to his throat. He'd shaved that morning, yet the lightest of stubble had already regrown, tickling her palms. She smoothed the tip of her index finger over his lips, outlining them. He nipped at her flesh with his teeth and she placed the tip of her finger into his mouth, grinning when his breathing grew progressively more ragged.

Her breasts already ached for the freedom to float free of her swimsuit. She almost gave in to the urge to strip. But she wanted *him* naked first. She wanted him as vulnerable, as open to her as she would soon be to him.

First she intended to familiarize her skin with his. Ryker's shoulders had fascinated her from the moment they'd met, and she smoothed the ridged musculature with light sweeping strokes that teased her palms with subtle friction. In contrast to her softness, his body was firm and warm. Warmer than the water. Warm enough to radiate heat through her hands, straight to her core.

At her boldness, at her enjoyment in discovering his sensitive places, her breasts ached and her nipples hardened into tiny buds that poked through the thin material of her swimsuit. She ignored her response, letting her imagination run wild as her hands roamed freely over his chest.

Impressed by his physique, her mouth went dry.

Her voice came out husky. "You know what I'm going to do to you?"

"What?"

"I'm going to rub my breasts against you. Would that be all right with you?"

His hands tightened around the rim. "That would be…fine."

With a knowing grin of satisfaction, she told him exactly what she intended to do before she moved. "I'll have to part my legs."

He groaned. Trembled. But didn't move.

And she'd never felt quite so sexy. After changing her position, she became aware that his sex had grown hard, strained beneath the swimsuit, and she found the idea of him ready and waiting for her a complete turn-on.

She straddled his hips, pressing lightly against his erection, knowing she could tease all she wanted and the tiny scrap of swimsuit between her legs would prevent him from going further than she was ready to permit. Though admittedly, she was ready to permit quite a lot. Then she leaned forward and brushed the tips of her breasts against him in a circular motion, like a cat in pursuit of a pleasurable caress.

And he groaned again, back arching to close the distance between them, chest muscles straining to feel more of her. "Do you have any idea what you're doing to me?"

"Is that a complaint?"

"No, just a question."

The water swirled around them, giving her freedom to move, to gyrate her hips without breaking the friction of her chest against his or halt the delicious sensations coursing through her. When she leaned forward to kiss his mouth, she intended to go slowly, lightly, but she couldn't hold back.

She discovered that the wait had increased her craving for his mouth. Her tongue tangled with his, mimicking the movements of her hips, until she'd wound her arms around his neck, threaded her fingers through his thick dark hair and plastered herself against him.

The thin material that separated their bodies had become a barrier. She craved the feel of his skin next to hers. Reaching down, she slipped her hands inside the waistband of his trunks. He lifted his hips, and she slid the material to his knees before returning to her former position.

"What about your suit?" he asked.

"Later." She reclaimed his mouth and let her hands explore his chest, his stomach, lower.

She traced his sex with her fingertips, enjoying his length and width, but most of all liking the way he leaped eagerly beneath her touch, causing an answering heat between her thighs. And she was far from done. He'd given her the opportunity to explore him at her leisure and she intended to make the most of her good fortune.

Sweat beaded on his forehead. "If you keep that up much longer, there isn't going to be a later."

"Just another few minutes."

"But—"

"No begging." She covered his mouth with hers and continued to touch him, enjoying the power of setting the pace. She'd wanted control over something in her life and he'd given her what she wanted without hesitation. She pulled back from the kiss and promised, "I'm going to give you everything you want."

She stood before him, the water up to her waist. "Don't move, except to open your eyes."

He did as she asked, the heat of his stare warming her straight to her toes. Then, ever so slowly, she eased her thumbs under the straps of her swimsuit. Her gaze focused on his, she peeled her swimsuit down slowly, revealing the swell of her breasts, then her areolae and finally her entire torso.

His breath grew into a rasp of need and her nipples tightened and extended until she ached. He was willing, eager. She could see the need for her in his eyes.

"You can wait just a little longer, can't you?" she coaxed.

His eyes challenged her. "If you make it worth my while."

"I might," she responded, so hot, so tense, so full of need she didn't know if she could keep going.

His Adam's apple bobbed in his throat as he swallowed hard. "You're going to push me over the edge."

"Not if you don't move." She lowered herself into the water then slowly raised herself until her breasts were at his eye level. She teased him by coming just a little closer. "Do you want to know what I like?"

Chapter Nine

"Show me." Ryker wasn't going to move and interrupt Daria's seduction—even if it killed him. At least he'd die a happy man.

Daria scooped up a handful of water, tilted back her head and poured the water over her neck and breasts. The water trickled downward, leaving a wet trail on her delicate neck, elegant collarbone and delectable breasts. Water droplets clung to the tips of her pink nipples. His throat went dry and he knew only licking her beckoning flesh would quench his thirst.

Every male instinct told him to release his hands, which were gripping the pool's edge. Every male instinct built into human beings over the last million years cried out for him to go to her. But he fought down the primitive urge with a savage moan.

This was Daria's moment. And he wouldn't deny her one nanosecond.

He'd long gone past aching for her. She had a lovely body, but it was her spirit that turned him on. She'd let loose her sexuality in a way so explosive, so powerful that she held him captive with her need.

Her need to take control. Her need to be in charge of her own destiny for one moment in her chaotic life.

So he'd willingly given himself to her, recognizing that she needed not just sexual release but a reaffirmation of life. He gritted his teeth and watched in awe as she revealed the passionate woman she usually kept so well hidden.

She was sensuality incarnate. So alive. And he wanted her more than he could ever remember wanting anyone or anything.

Finally she approached him and reached for the towel she'd left by the edge of the whirlpool. For one terrible moment he feared she was going to leave him there, hanging on by his nails to his sanity. But then she held up a foil packet, ripped it open between her teeth and removed a lubricated condom.

"Where did that come from?" he asked.

"I wouldn't be sharing this tub with you if I hadn't already made preparations." She patted the edge of the pool and he lifted himself out of the water, pleased to know that her feelings weren't spur-of-the-moment—but planned.

In absolutely no rush, she gazed at all he had to offer and fondled him before she unrolled the protection over his sex and tugged him back into the water.

Without hesitation, she climbed into his lap, and when she slowly lowered her hips, finally allowing him inside her, he had to bite his lip not to shout his appreciation. The delicious wait had made him crazy with need.

Finally he could touch her. And he wanted to do everything at once. He placed his hands on her back, her bottom, her waist. Her skin was so soft, so silky, like slick satin, that he didn't think he could ever get enough.

He dipped his head and finally sipped the water from her breasts. She tasted like nectar from the gods, sweet and hot. And when he lifted his head and looked into eyes dilated with passion, she grabbed his shoulders and slanted her mouth over his.

And then she rode him, hot and hard, her hips pumping to their own rhythm, her breath rasping, their tongues dueling. He slipped one hand between her thighs, caressed her and urged her to take him wherever she wanted to go.

She shuddered in release, but she didn't stop riding him and he didn't stop playing. She wanted to go longer and somehow he stayed with her.

Blood pumped through his veins. Every muscle clenched in need. His lungs burned with the effort to wait. But he never allowed his fingers to lose the beat.

Then she spasmed, shouted his name. No words ever sounded so hot. And he could hold back no longer. He gathered her close and held on tight while pure sensation washed over him, blessed release that went on and on until he relaxed in mellow wonder.

It took a few minutes for him to recover. He pulled her close, tucked her head under his chin. "You were fantastic."

She refused to meet his gaze for the first time since climbing into the tub. "I went too far."

"You were wonderful. Incredible. Awesome."

She trembled in his arms. "You're the one who deserves the compliments…"

He chuckled. "Okay. We're both terrific."

"I've never…"

"All that matters is that we enjoyed ourselves."

She leaned back to look him in the eye. "Is enjoying ourselves really all that matters?"

Uh-oh. He didn't want to go there. Delving into feelings wasn't his thing. When he didn't answer, she snuggled against him.

She didn't say another word, but he could have sworn he could hear her brain circuits humming. With another woman he would have settled for silence, perhaps urged her into another bout of lovemaking. But with Daria, he found himself oddly curious about what she was thinking. And while he was content to ignore his growing feelings for her, he didn't want her to do the same, but wasn't sure why.

Despite knowing that it was in his best interest to keep his mouth shut, he asked, "What are you thinking?"

"That we aren't right for one another."

"You could have fooled me."

"I meant in the long term."

Uh-oh. Again, he had no idea what to say. So for a response, he grunted.

Naturally she took that as the go-ahead. "I know it's the trend these day to have sex and then fall in love or not—but that's never been my style."

"So I'm the exception?" In one way he felt proud but in another disconcerted. And deep in his heart, where emptiness had once ruled, new feelings bloomed.

"I just don't…"

"Make wild, passionate love with a stranger?"

She frowned at him. "You aren't exactly a stranger. We've spent lots of time together, compressed time. It's just that I learned a long time ago not to get serious about men like you."

"What do you mean? Men like me?"

"You don't own a plant or a pet."

He hadn't a clue what she was saying. "Let me get this straight. You don't make love to men who don't own plants or a dog?"

Her expressive face took on a stoic look. "That's right."

He didn't get it. That's what he got for trying to understand the female mind. He should have been happy that she wanted him, but for reasons he didn't understand, lovemaking alone didn't satisfy him. He wanted more from this woman than lovemaking. He wanted to know what she thought, but she was speaking in riddles.

"Am I going to have to call my sister to ask her what you mean?"

She sighed at him as if he were denser than lead. "Men who don't have time for pets and plants don't want permanent relationships."

"We don't?" She sure was reading a lot into his personality from one measly visit to his apartment. He was thinking he would enjoy her company for a long time, months, maybe years.

"What's the longest relationship you've ever had?" she asked, her eyes both sad and mischievous.

"Two, three months," he admitted, knowing she would hold that information against him, but he wasn't yet ready to tell her that she was different, not when he barely understood his reactions himself. So he made a simple excuse. "My work tends to get in the way."

"How convenient."

How had they gone from the most incredible love-making of his life to this absurd conversation? And why was he already thinking that being together this one time would never be enough? "Are we fighting?"

She splashed him. "Not as long as you agree with me."

DARIA WOKE UP in the middle of the night and found Ryker in front of his computer screen. She knew he was eager to do some research, but she hadn't realized he'd intended to work through the night.

She came up behind him and peered over his shoulder at a series of commands that she didn't understand. "Have you gotten any sleep?"

"A combat nap."

"What's that?"

He kept typing as he spoke. "Fifteen minutes of deep REM sleep. It's surprisingly refreshing. With a lot of practice I've learned to fall asleep immediately. Saves time."

She had to admit he didn't look tired. His fingers danced in a blur over the keyboard, and he was carrying on a conversation with her at the same time.

Since her questions didn't interfere with his work, she saw no reason not to satisfy her curiosity. "Have you found anything useful?"

"I've been e-mailing the Shey Group with requests."

She pulled over an extra chair to sit beside him. "What kind of requests?"

"Logan Kincaid has contacts at the CIA. I want him to find out about Harry's last missions."

She didn't understand. Maybe she was still groggy. "Wouldn't the recent poisoning of Elizabeth and Peter discount the theory that someone had been after Harry?"

"Probably. But I like to tie up all the loose ends. Suppose an agent killed Harry and Fallon then framed you to take off the heat. Since you haven't been arrested and the case is still open, maybe one more killing would make them appear completely blameless, and you completely guilty."

"I see." She did. In the world he lived in, nothing was what it seemed. He had to look at every detail, suspect every clue as if it might be a false one.

He cracked his knuckles then went back to typing. "I wanted to do this from your office. But my machine encrypts ingoing and outgoing e-mail and makes decoding almost impossible for anyone unless they work for the Pentagon."

She tightened the belt of her bathrobe. "You still think the altered e-mail message on my computer about Passion Perfect's toxicity to my supplier had something to do with the murders?"

He nodded. "That your computer disappeared from the police evidence room makes me even more suspicious."

''Weren't you going to get a copy from my Internet service provider?''

''I requested the information.''

''And?''

''They won't cooperate without a warrant.''

''So now what?'' She tried to keep the frustration from her voice but it wasn't easy. Everywhere they turned seemed to lead to a dead end.

''I asked Kincaid how he wants me to proceed.''

''What are the choices?''

''He can get me the warrant…or I can hack in.''

''Isn't that illegal?'' She didn't want him taking risks for her, not the kind that could put him in jail or make him lose his job.

Ryker stopped typing and faced her. ''It's as illegal as double-parking. I won't get caught—''

''Because you're good?''

''Because I was taught by one of the best in the business.''

''And who might that be?''

''Logan Kincaid.'' So much for the possibility of him getting caught and losing his job. Not if his boss was the one who'd taught him. ''And he's one of the good guys,'' Ryker reassured her.

''But suppose you *do* get caught?''

''I won't damage any Web sites. And I'm not selling the information. When no harm is done, the penalty's a slap on the wrist. Nothing more.''

''But you'll wait to hear from Kincaid?''

His computer beeped, signaling an incoming message.

She read the message from his boss off the screen.

"It's midnight. No point waking a judge when you can get in. Good Luck. LK."

Ryker started typing. Different screens came up and disappeared so quickly that she had no idea what he was doing. "Are you writing a code to break in?"

"I'm using one that's already written and stored in a vault. Once I extract the worm, I just have to sit back and wait."

She suspected it wasn't as easy as he claimed and wondered just how many people in the world had his kind of specialized expertise.

The site asked him for a password but he didn't even touch the keypad. Whatever he'd set in motion seemed to work of its own accord.

Then Ryker clapped his hands together and rubbed them. "We're in."

She had no idea if his task was now simple or complex, but suspected the latter. "Aren't there millions of messages stored in there?"

"Yes. But every account has a number and the e-mails are dated. However, I'm going to search for 'Passion Perfect' and the date of the e-mail from the police report."

The screen read "Searching."

He opened a new panel, called up another search engine and typed "Harrington Industries." A flood of references filled the screen.

Apparently his computer was sophisticated enough to handle more than one search at a time, but the topic took her aback. "Why are you looking into my father's company?"

"Curiosity. Do you think Shandra really needed the money she borrowed?"

Maybe Ryker hadn't been getting enough sleep. Maybe making love had scrambled his brains. "You can't believe that my father is killing his children because he needs money? Or that Shandra would go along with it?"

"I don't know. That's why I'm searching. I think it's more likely that Mike Brannigan's our guy. But your family's business operations are extensive. It may take my computer days to search through the pertinent data. So it makes sense to start with the most complicated businesses first."

He *was* making sense. She just had so little knowledge of his area of expertise. She'd known he was smart, but she hadn't realized that when he focused, he could be intense and talk to her at the same time. His multitasking ability was extraordinary. He could carry on a complex conversation and still type over a hundred words a minute.

She supposed there were lots of things she didn't know about Ryker. But she knew the most important thing—she wanted him on her side. And not just because he had a brilliant mind and might solve the problem she found herself facing. He seemed to understand her feelings without her making explanations. He'd understood that her need to make love with him had more to do with her distress and need for comfort and human connection than any special relationship between them.

Not that she didn't admire Ryker. She did. But under normal circumstances, she would never have made love to a man with whom she had so little in common. It wasn't money or social class that made them incompatible. From what Harry's attorney had told her, the men in the Shey Group were all millionaires several times over.

And she didn't consider the way she'd grown up superior to anyone's upbringing. Her life had been loveless. Without Fallon and then Peter, she might not have survived whole.

However, the men she had dated were conservative businessmen, who were risk-adverse. Men who liked stability as much as she did. Men who stayed in one place.

While Ryker made acquaintances easily, she suspected he didn't have one close friend. He didn't stay in one place long enough to form those kind of long-term attachments. And she sensed a loneliness in him that made her wary.

"What's the computer looking for now?"

"Breaks in a pattern. The program is preset to look at bank statements. Suppose your father gives Shandra ten thousand dollars a month, every month for household expenses. But if he skips February, my program will notice."

"It's looking at my family's bank statements?"

"And phone bills, credit card bills, income tax statements, driving records, criminal records, military records. It can go back and tell me where someone was born, their grades in college and where they married."

"I had no idea you could find all that information online."

"The difficult part isn't acquiring the information but sorting through the data and figuring out what is important and what's not. I've given the program certain parameters. Any contact with the law will come up. As will bankruptcies."

"How…" She wasn't even sure what to ask.

"Each category is given a number. Previous convictions and arrest records are number one. If my program finds that information, it will list it first. But then I altered the parameters of the search for your case."

"Can you give me an example?"

"Sure. If Mike Brannigan took out a library book on poisons, that fact will go to the top of my list."

"This is amazing."

"Helpful, yes, extraordinary, maybe, but don't expect the computer to solve the case for us. The computer's a tool that's going to give us masses of data. But it takes the human brain to take the data, analyze it and put the important pieces together."

Suddenly the machine beeped. Ryker closed one screen and opened another. He frowned then turned to her with a tight expression on his lips.

"What's wrong?"

"Your ISP came up empty."

"You mean the police were mistaken about the altered e-mail on my computer?"

"There are possibilities. Either the hacker remembered to cover his tracks with your Internet provider and erased the data—"

"Or?"

"A hacker altered the e-mail on just your hard drive."

"What does that mean?"

"It means…that either way, we're dealing with someone with above-average computer abilities."

"Which means we can probably eliminate Shandra and Isabelle." Glum, she leaned back in her chair. "So that leaves the rest of my employees, Sam, Jeanie and Cindy."

"Mike Brannigan and your father, but even I don't think your father poisoned Fallon and Peter."

"Have you heard back from Logan Kincaid about Harry's assignments?"

Ryker spun in his chair. "Let me check." He struck a few keys. "Nothing yet. But I'm getting some early hits from the search engines."

"Anything interesting?"

"So far Mike Brannigan's clean. Sam doesn't have a criminal record, but he has been arrested."

"My bookkeeper, Sam? That's hard to believe. Are you sure?"

"Apparently they suspected him of racketeering."

"Sam?" She couldn't believe it. He was just a college kid. "What's racketeering?"

"It covers a wide range of white-collar criminal activity. We'll ask him about it tomorrow."

"We're closed on Sundays."

"Then we can pay him a visit." He perused the data on the screen. "Cindy just bought a house. Put down a large down payment."

"That's odd."

"Why?"

She stared at the numbers on the screen. "She didn't say anything to me about it. And I don't pay her enough for her to save that kind of down payment."

"Maybe we should go talk to Cindy first. Didn't you say she recently returned from a vacation near the greenhouse that burned down?"

"Yes, but—"

Ryker busily typed. "Her bank account shows a sudden hefty deposit made two weeks before Fallon's death."

"A payoff?" Or a coincidence? Daria had absolutely no idea.

"Some people will do anything for money. Even commit murder."

CINDY PARKS LIVED in an apartment that she shared with two other twentysomething single females. Old and renovated, the building still smelled of dust despite the freshly painted walls and shiny floors.

As Ryker escorted Daria into the lobby and up on the elevator, he had difficulty keeping his mind on his computer search. Daria was wearing a soft pink blouse and a simple gray skirt that ended at midthigh and attracted his gaze like a bee to pollen. He kept thinking about their lovemaking, her legs tucked over his. He was pretty sure that Daria wanted to forget they'd ever made love, that she didn't want to attach any special significance to what they'd done, but he wanted to remember every lusty moment. Just the recollection of her breasts made him hard all over again. Her sensuality hadn't just stunned him, it had swept him away in a thundercloud of desire he'd never forget.

"Ryker?"

From the tone of Daria's voice he figured that she'd called his names several times and he hadn't heard until now.

"Yeah."

"How do we justify interrupting Cindy's Sunday morning?"

"We don't."

Daria had wanted to call first. But he didn't want Cindy to prepare for their questions. He wanted her off guard.

"Apartment 4B. Here we are."

Ryker rang the bell and slipped his arm through Daria's. He liked having an excuse to touch her. Liked breathing in her sweet scent, liked the feel of her against his side. And he especially liked the warm feeling that accompanying her gave him.

A sleepy-eyed redhead answered the door. When she recognized Daria, she stepped back, her eyes widening with surprise. "Ms. Harrington? And you must be Ryker Stevens, the new accountant."

Ryker took the open door as an invitation to enter. The messy apartment reeked of old wine, stale pizza and smoke. Yesterday's newspaper lay on the couch, one page neatly folded to the story of Elizabeth's death and Peter's close escape. Cindy saw him notice the article and she turned white.

Her reaction didn't fit. Why was she worried that they'd caught her reading about Harrington Bouquet's employee and someone she probably knew? Curiosity was normal. That she wanted to conceal her curiosity probably meant she had something to hide, but what?

"We wanted to ask you a few questions," Daria told her designer and head of customer service.

"The police already did." Cindy's voice raised in defiance. "I haven't done anything wrong."

"Of course you haven't," Ryker told her, trying to calm her defensiveness. "We were just wondering about the purchase of your house."

Cindy frowned at him then looked to Daria for an explanation. "Excuse me? I don't understand."

"You never told me about buying a house," Daria prodded gently.

"You never asked."

"Are you moving into the suburbs?" Daria asked.

"I haven't decided. I may just rent the place to cover the payments."

Ryker made his voice hard, hoping she'd answer without thinking too much. "Where did you get the money for the down payment?"

"That's none of your business," Cindy snapped, her posture defensive.

"Maybe. Maybe not. If that down payment was a payoff—"

"For what? Murder? You think I…" Cindy threw her arms into the air in disgust. "Why would I poison—"

"For money?" Ryker pushed her harder.

"That's ridiculous."

"Why don't you just tell us where you got the down payment and you can avoid the police coming back here to ask you all over again,'' Ryker suggested.

Cindy crossed her arms over her chest and glared at him. ''I don't have to answer your questions.''

''I was hoping you'd help me out because you wanted to.'' Daria spoke softly. ''I only came here so I could narrow down the suspects and cross you off the list. You have to admit the big down payment in your bank account two weeks before my sister's death looks suspicious.''

''How do you know what's in my bank account?'' Cindy countered.

Ryker took out his cell phone. ''Look, you can cooperate, or I can call Detective O'Brien, and you can explain everything to him.''

Cindy looked from him to Daria again as if her boss was going to help her out. ''If you must know, I inherited the money from my great-aunt.''

''What's her name?'' Ryker asked.

''Ruth Ann Semore.'' Cindy looked him straight in the eye. ''She died about a year ago, and it took this long for her estate to go through probate.''

Daria sounded both puzzled and hurt. ''How come you never mentioned your windfall or the house?''

''Because I didn't want you to think that just because I might move out of the city I wouldn't be working the same hours.''

Cindy had been afraid of losing her job? Ryker didn't buy it. And something bothered him about her statement.

As they left Cindy's building and headed toward

Daria's car, he spoke his doubts aloud. "Cindy didn't want me going to the police."

"Maybe she doesn't want them to know she smokes pot. I saw a five-leafed plant in the corner…"

"Maybe. But I saw Cindy's tax returns. I can't be positive without another look, but I think that last year she reported a gift from the estate."

Daria squeezed his hand tightly. "So she inherited the money?"

"Yes. But the amount she reported to the IRS was about ten times smaller than the down payment on her home." He'd bet his new hard drive that Cindy Parks was lying.

Chapter Ten

Content to let Ryker drive her car, Daria leaned back and closed her eyes. She didn't enjoy investigating the personal lives of her employees, but she liked even less the idea of spending the rest of her life in jail for a crime she didn't commit. Yet, even if she proved her innocence, she suspected some of her business relationships might never again be the same.

Her life would never be the same again without her sister. But it would be an added burden to discover they'd been betrayed by an employee and a friend.

And Cindy's attitude had been downright hostile. Without Ryker's steady presence beside her, she might not have had the guts to shoulder her way inside. She would have backed off the conversation much earlier, and she certainly wouldn't have questioned Cindy about the down payment. Daria would have been more focused on assuring her employee that commuting into the city would be fine with her as long as it didn't affect Cindy's job performance.

Daria had to stop thinking like the businesswoman she was and figure out who had killed the people closest to her. Her mind kept skittering away from the subject, just as it did when she thought about making love to Ryker. While she didn't exactly regret her actions, she didn't want to think about her feelings either.

She much preferred to believe that making love to him had been an aberration in her behavior that she could just remember fondly, and that meant nothing important. Only, she couldn't forget the way his hands had felt on her bottom, or how the heat in his eyes had made her feel so feminine. She absolutely didn't even want to consider that maybe the great sex had been because her feelings toward Ryker were changing.

Her cell phone rang, and she almost didn't answer, but she feared Peter could have taken a turn for the worse. He'd hurt her badly when he'd refused to speak to her, but at least he hadn't openly accused her of trying to poison him. *Yet.*

Opening her eyes, she plucked the phone out of her purse. ''Hello?''

''Can you meet me at Sour Pickles in twenty minutes?'' Mike Brannigan's voice sounded harried, and she hit the speaker option so Ryker could listen. She knew Ryker wanted to pop in unexpectedly on Sam next, but Mike was also a suspect, and he sounded determined to talk to her.

''I'm running a few errands. Can this wait?'' she asked. Strange how she no longer found the executive attractive. Compared to Ryker, he was downright annoying, even if they did share similar interests, even if they did hang out in the same social circles.

''It's important.''

She restrained a sigh of exasperation. "Can't you tell me over the phone?"

"I'd rather not."

Did he think someone was listening? Who?

Beside her, Ryker nodded agreement and she changed her mind. "Okay, Mike. We'll be there—"

"Who's we?" Mike's voice rose with suspicion.

"Ryker and me."

"Fine. See you in twenty."

Daria dropped the phone back into her purse. "He sounded odd. Mike is usually smooth and charming. Not much throws him off center." And he hadn't seemed to mind that Ryker would be accompanying her—so *who* hadn't he wanted to come with her?

Ryker smoothly avoided a jaywalker. "Any chance Cindy might have just called Mike?"

"Why?"

"Well, if she didn't inherit all that money from her great-aunt like she claims, maybe Mike Brannigan paid her off."

"I don't think they know one another."

"According to computer records, Mike and Cindy are first cousins."

"I didn't know. Can you find out who wrote the check she deposited into her account?"

"That kind of digging is tough, but it can be done." Ryker turned left at the light and merged into traffic. "Mike could have offered a stranger a bribe, but it's odd that neither one of them ever mentioned their relationship to you. Her mother's brother is his father."

She sighed. "It seems there's a lot I don't know

about my employees.'' And a lot she didn't know about herself. She found the entire situation upsetting, uncomfortable and distasteful. But the necessity of continuing the investigation kept her from voicing her opinion.

While Daria wasn't naive enough to believe that people were always just what they seemed, she found it unsettling to learn that no one was what she'd first believed. Not even Ryker. When she'd hired him, she thought she'd get the tough, military type. She hadn't considered that he had a gentle side, a playful side or that he could be so considerate about her feelings.

And she hadn't figured on becoming so attached to him or so comfortable around him. He had a quiet way of showing support and yet he never failed to step in with an air of command when the situation warranted it. However, he was just as comfortable sitting back and allowing her to take charge, like holding completely still while she seduced him.

She still couldn't believe she'd acted so boldly. And yet, she'd felt at ease doing so with him. While she wanted to blame her behavior on stress, she suspected that was a cop-out. But with everything else going on, she couldn't handle delving too deeply into her own fragile feelings. Normally she would have saved those kinds of thoughts to share with Fallon or Elizabeth. At the double loss her heart clenched with grief and she renewed her determination to find their killer.

Ahead of them a taxi cut off a garbage truck. Ryker swerved to the right to avoid the fender bender. He seemed terribly eager to get through the intersection.

As the light turned from green to yellow to red, he stepped on the gas, then checked his rearview mirror.

She released her death grip on the door. "We really have plenty of time. Despite Mike's impatience, he'll wait if we're a few minutes late."

"See that champagne sedan behind us?"

She started to turn in her seat and her gray skirt notched up an inch. She tugged it down.

"Use the mirror," he instructed. "That car went through the red light, and he's changed lanes several times right after we did."

She would never have noticed. But now a chill shimmied down her back. "You think that car is following us?"

"This might be the break we need."

She was trying not to voice her fears, but he sounded pleased with the danger, like a kid who'd just unwrapped a special Christmas toy. "What are you talking about?"

"I'm going to stop short at the next light. I'll get out and take a look. See who's driving."

"That's the dumbest plan I've ever heard," she muttered. "Why can't you check the license plate?"

"It's in the rear. That car isn't going to let me slip behind him."

"Suppose they shoot you?"

"I'm glad to hear you're worried about me. I was beginning to think you didn't care."

"If you die on me, hiring another investigator will be inconvenient—and besides, I'll probably get blamed for your murder."

"How touching."

"I'm nixing your plan."

He raised an eyebrow, and she could tell he was quite amused. "Really?"

"I hired you. You take orders from me."

"Darling, you just go on believing that if it makes you feel better."

His patronizing tone irritated her. She grabbed her cell phone from her purse, checked the number on the business card the detective had given her, then dialed. She spoke in a rush, relieved that the next few lights stayed green and that Ryker continued to drive.

"Detective O'Brien, this is Daria Harrington. There's a champagne-colored car tailing us down Forty-Second Street."

"No need to worry, Ms. Harrington. I'm following you." His tone sounded sheepish and wry. "And I'd appreciate it if you didn't run any more red lights."

She lifted the phone up to Ryker's mouth. This time she heard a definite chuckle. Damn him for enjoying himself when her stomach remained in knots.

"Learning anything useful, Detective?" Ryker asked dryly.

"It occurred to me that if someone killed Daria's sister, and tried to kill her brother, that same someone might also come after her."

Daria took back the phone and spoke into the speaker. "So kind of you to be concerned about me, Detective. Any luck on finding my missing computer from the evidence room?"

"Not yet. You might be interested in knowing that your brother refused police protection."

"And why would I find that interesting? I already know we Harringtons like our privacy."

"Since he survived, I just thought that maybe the killer might try again."

"You really think Peter's in danger?"

"The real question is…what do you think? Is your brother in danger?"

His implication was clear. He was asking her if she intended to try to poison Peter again.

Angry, Daria hung up the phone, convinced that the detective was following her to catch her trying to kill her brother. Obviously Ryker's credentials only went so far. If the detective was tailing them, he couldn't be looking for the real killer.

"Don't pay attention to him," Ryker told her. "He's just doing his job."

The Sour Pickle was a tiny delicatessen crowded with tourists and shoppers on their lunch hour. The smells of freshly baked bread and salami made Ryker's mouth water. For some reason, being around Daria spiked his appetite for food and for sex. He wanted her again, wished they could forget about this meeting, go back to her place and spend the afternoon in her whirlpool. The truth was he didn't want to share her with Mike. He wanted to keep her to himself.

The jealousy jarred him. He couldn't ever remember feeling this way about another woman.

But with Daria, he didn't want just sex. He liked being around her. Enjoyed sharing her home, her conversation, her time. When he thought back on his life, he realized that he hadn't known until now how empty it had been. Between intense missions traveling with the Shey Group, he'd spent the majority of his time on his computer. His hobby had turned into a career that had separated him from close human contact outside the Shey Group and prevented him from making friends, casual or otherwise.

He now thought of his pre-Daria time as lonely, a place to which he had no intention of returning. That his decision couldn't be unilateral bothered him. Daria needed his investigative skills and she'd enjoyed their lovemaking, but he had no idea how she really felt about him. And he doubted she knew, herself. The woman was guarded about her emotions, closed up. But that would make the reward of convincing her that she had deeper feelings for him all the more challenging. And Ryker did love a good challenge. All he had to do now was decide on a plan—one that would convince Daria that she wasn't just responding to him because he happened to be handy, but because they were good together.

On the surface they seemed so different. But after spending time with her, he realized that they had more in common than he'd ever have believed possible. Both of them took their work and their commitments seriously. They both did their jobs to the best of their abilities, and both of them tended to focus on work instead of their private lives. He figured they meshed nicely. Even when he left for other missions, Daria would have her work.

For the first time, he admitted to himself he was falling in love with her. And he was smart enough to know that what he felt was special. But he had his work cut out for him. Daria didn't seem too inclined to return his feelings. However, he did like a woman who presented a challenge.

Beside him, Daria didn't even glance at the glass case full of cold cuts, salads and pastries. Her gaze went straight toward the rear where Mike Brannigan had commandeered a corner table. He'd stood the moment Ryker and Daria came through the door, but Mike also took a good look at Daria's legs before raising his eyes to greet them. And Ryker didn't like the man noticing her legs—not one damn bit.

Ryker had had more difficulty finding parking than he'd had shaking O'Brien off his tail, so they'd arrived several minutes late. And from the impatient look on Mike Brannigan's face, he didn't like to be kept waiting. The knowledge that Daria had a history with Brannigan shouldn't have bothered Ryker. In his past relationships he'd never cared who had come before him or who came after him. But with Daria, he wondered if she still had feelings for the man. She'd only told him that when Mike had displayed as much interest in her business as in her, she'd broken off seeing him. Had Mike hurt her?

Ryker thrust the disturbing thought from his mind. Her personal past had nothing to do with him. And he couldn't allow himself to be distracted from the case.

Mike leaned forward to hug Daria but she offered him her hand instead. After the two men shook hands and seated themselves, a waitress immediately approached and they gave their orders.

"What's wrong, Mike?" Daria asked the moment the waitress left. However, her tone was calm, almost as if she suspected this meeting was simply another attempt for Mike to convince her to sell him her business.

Mike kept his voice low. "How strong is Harrington Industries right now?"

Not Harrington Bouquet, but Harrington Industries—her father's company—the one Peter was being groomed to run.

Ryker had to give Daria credit. When it came to business, she had the best poker face he'd ever seen. That really threw him, because in her personal life he found her much easier to read. But she gave nothing away. No hint that Shandra had come to her asking for a loan or that things might not be going so well with her father's business.

Daria calmly picked up a sesame seed bread stick. "What have you heard?"

For once Ryker fully appreciated her method of attacking when she felt defensive. Although she had to be eaten up with curiosity, by her stoic expression, she could have been discussing the weather.

And he was much relieved not to feel any male-female subtext between her and Mike. If the two were ever involved, they were obviously finished.

"The powers that be at Homemart think Harrington Industries is ripe for a hostile takeover."

Daria shrugged. "Amicron's hostile takeover bid failed last year. And Dunstan Limited tried and failed two years before that."

"Yeah." Mike lowered his voice even more. "But

now there are rumors that your father's company has cooked their books. That they're cash starved. Vulnerable.''

"Every major company has faced those kinds of rumors since Enron collapsed. It's not like you to believe them. And I don't understand why you're so concerned that you had to interrupt our weekend.''

Mike ignored Daria's implication that Ryker and she were together, having a pleasurable day until he'd interrupted them. Ryker knew otherwise. The meeting with Cindy had upset Daria more than she'd admitted.

Mike leaned forward, his face intense. "Because this is different. Ware's on the board of directors at Homemart.''

Interesting. Ryker plucked a pickle from the tiny bucket on the table and crunched away while he thought hard. The name of the D.A., her father's enemy, kept turning up in the unlikeliest of places. Ryker made a mental note to add the man to his computer search. Although he couldn't picture the prominent district attorney planting evidence against Daria, he certainly had the power to make her computer disappear from the police evidence room.

Daria pointed at Mike with her bread stick. "And why are you telling me this?''

Mike slapped the table with his palm, causing the water glasses to quiver. "Because Ware doesn't just want Harrington Industries. He wants Harrington Bouquet, too.''

And Mike also wanted Harrington Bouquet. Maybe this was another meeting to try to convince Daria to sell Mike the business. He certainly was persistent, but was he dangerous?

He couldn't have determined from Mike's sophistication now that he had grown up on the rough side of town. From the superficial background check, Ryker knew Brannigan had attended Ivy League schools and taken some computer courses, but that meant nothing. Many people were self-taught hackers. He had no military background either, but he'd known enough not to talk on the telephone.

Daria placed her bread stick down. "I'm a private corporation. No one can force me to sell. And my bank has said nothing about the morals clause."

"But what if Ware puts you in jail? The bank will certainly be concerned then about your company's debt. Won't you have to sell then?"

"Maybe. Maybe not."

"Did it ever occur to you that if you sold Harrington Bouquet to me you wouldn't be such a large and attractive target for Ware to come after?"

Daria leaned back in disgust. "I don't want to hear this."

Mike turned to Ryker, his eyes gleaming with fervor. "Make her listen to reason. Sure, I want the company, but I think Ware wants it more. And despite how things ended between Daria and me, I don't want her to end up in jail."

Mike had made his case with a zealous intensity. But he hadn't given them one fact they could check. Ryker didn't operate on rumors. He needed hard evidence.

"Care to tell us where you came by this information?" Ryker asked.

"No. I don't."

Ryker picked up a sour tomato and nibbled. "Why not?"

"Because I'm already jeopardizing my career by telling you what I know."

"You expect me to believe you came here out of the kindness of your heart?"

"I've made no secret that I want to buy Harrington Bouquet. The acquisition would be a coup for my company. I'd probably get a bonus from my grandfather and maybe a promotion. However, I'm also concerned over Daria."

Daria spoke quietly, but her tone left no doubt about her displeasure that the two men's discussion was going on as if she weren't there. "I'll take care of myself. And my company."

Mike rolled his eyes at the ceiling. "Fine." He threw a few bills down on the table to cover the lunch he apparently had no intention of eating. "Just remember that I warned you."

He stalked off just as the waitress returned with their food. She frowned at the money, then looked to Ryker for an explanation.

He patted the empty place setting, indicating she should leave the extra sandwich. "He had to go. But now there's more for us."

Daria sighed and ignored her food. "I'm glad someone's hungry."

His mouth full, Ryker shrugged. When he could

again speak, he picked up her uneaten bread stick. "Mike's given us several more things to consider."

"You mean Ware?"

"Yeah, and I want to dig deeper into your father's company. But first, let's go see your bookkeeper."

SAM LIVED ALONE in an immaculate apartment on the Upper West Side. Daria had expected the student and bookkeeper to have roommates and live in a hovel, probably due to his age and the fact that he always acted as if he was broke. But when she thought about him she realized that Sam was tight. He never put quarters into the candy and soda machines. He brown-bagged his lunch. And she suspected he cut his own hair.

However, he had a great sound system, a flat-screen television and a pricey computer with a laser printer. On the kitchen counter was a two-line phone system, a set of keys and a pager. She knew his parents weren't paying for his college education, and he couldn't afford this place on what she paid him, so where did his money come from?

Sam welcomed them into his living area with a cheery grin, his eyes clear and friendly behind his thick glasses. He wore jeans and a Polo shirt and had a cell phone clipped to his belt.

"Come in." He puffed out his chest, proud of the place. "Cindy called and said you might be coming over."

So much for surprising him.

"Would you like something to drink?" he asked,

gesturing for them to take seats on his navy leather couch.

"No, thanks," Daria said.

"Nice system." Although Ryker's glance at the computer equipment might appear casual, Daria knew it was thorough, but she didn't have a clue what had caught his interest.

Sam's glasses slid onto his nose, and he pushed them back up. "Cool, huh?"

"How do you afford all this on a bookkeeper's salary?" Ryker got right to the point.

Sam grinned. "I'm day-trading. Doing pretty well for myself."

Daria already knew that Ryker would check out this information the moment they returned to her apartment. While Sam seemed open and much less harried than he was at work, he appeared almost overly friendly. At work, the kid she knew barely spoke to her other employees and appeared to have the social skills of a certified nerd, yet here on his home ground he seemed confident, almost boastful. And again she thought that no one was what they seemed.

Not even her. She pretended that she alone could handle her business and the stress of being the primary suspect in a murder investigation, but the truth was entirely different. She had come to depend on Ryker in ways she didn't want to acknowledge. But as much as she tried to deny her feelings, she could only distract herself for so long before they emerged again, each time stronger and more insistent.

During this interview with her employee, she

counted on Ryker to ask the right questions. But just as important, her emotional connection to Ryker gave her the strength to get through this ordeal.

Ryker straddled a stool. "The markets have been mostly down recently."

Sam shrugged. "Doesn't matter to me. I make money whether the stocks go up or down. I have a computer system…"

Ryker stood, and strode over to the blank computer screen. "You wrote a program that predicts the market? Can I see it?"

Sam shook his head. "Sorry. I'm going to write a book—after I make my fortune."

"So how come you're still working for me?" Daria asked, realizing that although she couldn't put her finger on what was bothering her, Sam's story didn't add up.

First Cindy and now Sam had more money than she'd thought possible. She would have considered embezzlement—except the wholesale end of her business was done by check and neither Sam nor Cindy had signing authority—only Daria could do that. And neither Sam nor Cindy could have funded their lifestyles with petty theft out of the retail cash drawer. Besides, neither of them had access.

Perhaps Cindy *had* inherited the money for the down payment on her home. Perhaps Sam *was* a wildly successful day trader. But why had Cindy called Sam to tell him they were on the way over? Obviously they knew one another better than Daria had thought. Before today she wouldn't have thought Cindy knew Sam's home phone number.

Sam's phone rang and his pager went off. He ignored both.

"Aren't you going to answer?" Daria asked.

"Voice mail will get it."

The moment the phone stopped ringing, it started again. Then line two lit up. Sam strode over to his phone and turned off the ringer.

Clearly he didn't want to talk in front of them. When his cell phone rang next, he reset it to vibrate. "Sorry about that."

While the phones were now silent, Daria could see the lights of the phone lines continue to light up. Daria shifted in her seat to watch Sam's eyes. "Sam, are you running your day trades for other people?"

"I don't have a license."

While he hadn't admitted culpability, he hadn't denied her allegation, either. Was that how Cindy had made her money? Had she given her inheritance to Sam to play with in the stock market? Was that why she'd called to warn him?

"Is that why you were arrested for racketeering?"

"How'd you find out about that? I was a juvenile. The records were supposed to be sealed."

She didn't answer and Ryker changed the subject. "Sam, how well did you know Elizabeth?"

"I didn't go into the store often. We said hello on the occasions we bumped into each other, that's it."

Fallon would have had no need for Sam's investment services. But Daria wondered if Elizabeth had known about Sam's sideline. "You never spoke with Elizabeth on the phone?"

"She was straitlaced. She kept her money in a

cookie jar. She wasn't interested in the market. In fact, she thought playing the market was gambling.''

So Sam had talked to her about investing money. So what? This was getting them nowhere. None of this could explain Harry's and Fallon's or Elizabeth's murders.

Ryker folded his arms across his chest, his voice firm. "All right, Sam. Either you come clean right now or I'm calling the police.''

Daria hadn't a clue where Ryker was going with this. But he looked fierce as hell and twice as dangerous.

Sam tried to stand up to Ryker but his eyes widened in fear. "What are you talking about?"

Ryker stood perfectly still and let his no-nonsense voice do his threatening for him. "Day traders need an Internet connection. You don't have one.''

Ryker's accusation shredded Sam's confident demeanor into tatters. The kid started to shake and he stammered, "D-don't call the c-cops.''

"Then don't lie to me.'' Ryker took one step in Sam's direction.

Sam cracked. "The day-trader thing is a cover.''

"For what?" Daria asked.

Sam stared at his shoes. "I lend money to people. And they pay me back more than they borrow. A lot more.''

Ryker took another step toward Sam, applying pressure. "You're a loan shark?"

Suddenly a few pieces of the puzzle fell into place for Daria. "You did business with Cindy?"

"She gave me the money she inherited so I could

lend it to someone else. She earned back her capital twenty times over and we split the profits.''

"Did my sister and her husband or Elizabeth have anything to do with your little scheme?" Daria asked.

"No. I swear it." Sam backed from Ryker toward Daria. "I just borrow and lend money. No one gets hurt."

Ryker's eyebrows rose in skepticism. "What happens when your clients can't repay their debts?"

"That's never happened."

"Never?"

"I've never had to do more than make a threatening phone call. I swear. It's easy money. Do I look like I could threaten anyone?"

Sam was about five foot five and a hundred and forty pounds. But he obviously had the funds to hire muscle. However, Daria couldn't see where their investigation was leading them. Sam's sideline seemed to have nothing to do with poison or murder or clearing her name.

Sam balanced the books for her and made extra money on the side. He knew little about flowers or poisons. He didn't even have one plant in his apartment. And even if Elizabeth had borrowed money from him, Sam couldn't collect from a dead person.

Sam wouldn't look her in the eye. "Are you going to turn me in?"

Chapter Eleven

Daria had told Sam that she wouldn't turn him in to the cops if he'd promise not to approach anyone in her business with his extracurricular schemes. Naturally, he'd agreed. But had her decision been a good one? She didn't know, and as much as she wanted to ask Ryker his opinion, she didn't. She didn't want turning to him to become a habit.

As she and Ryker drove back to her apartment, she had so much to think about. She always thought better at home where she eliminated outside distractions and created a soothing comfort zone. Ever since Fallon's and Harry's deaths, she'd found her personal retreat more necessary than ever.

If she went to jail, she'd lose her business, but more importantly she'd lose her home, which scared her right down to her toes. Her apartment was the center of her world, her safety net where she could withdraw and regroup.

She'd become accustomed to the idea of sharing her special place with Ryker in surprisingly short order. Maybe because he fit in so easily. The man adapted himself to new situations with a skill that amazed her. She imagined he would be as comfortable in a hammock or a submarine bunk as in a king-size bed. Harry's attorney had told her that Ryker's home was wherever he could plug in his computer.

But she wasn't comfy without her thick terry bathrobe and warm slippers, her cats curled in her lap and at her feet and a cup of hot tea within easy reach. Surrounding herself with her plants was like feeding her soul and as necessary as a daily shower.

So why were she and Ryker good together?

They had no possible future as a couple. Not when their lives were so dissimilar. For all practical purposes, Ryker was a mercenary, a soldier for hire. His work didn't allow him to put down roots. She wanted a man whose interests matched her own. A man who lived in one place. A man who didn't jeopardize his life on a daily basis. Yet, as she watched Ryker drive her car with relaxed concentration, his capable fingers on the wheel, she almost wished that he could adapt to her lifestyle on a permanent basis. Wished he could hang around long enough for them to give their relationship a chance to root. But when he finished helping her, he would be off to his next assignment in Kuwait or South Africa or Afghanistan.

She wouldn't choose a man like Ryker for a husband. Therefore she wouldn't allow herself to fall for him.

And why was she even thinking about the future when she didn't know if she had one? The D.A. could issue an arrest warrant for her any day. And murderers rarely got bail. For all she knew, these hours might be the last free ones she'd ever have. And they'd wasted the day talking to her employees and finding out absolutely nothing useful.

She must have grunted or sighed in frustration, because Ryker turned down the radio. "What?"

"I can't help but feeling that we're running out of time."

"I always feel that way when I'm on a case. Once I take on a mission, time speeds up. It's a natural law of the universe."

He sounded so happy. "And you enjoy living under this kind of pressure?"

"Doesn't everybody?"

He was completely serious. He enjoyed living on the edge. Indeed, confronting challenges and facing danger seemed to suit his personality. She gazed at him. His alert eyes were focused on the road, yet he constantly checked the rearview mirror for tails. And she had no doubt that after today's conversations with Cindy, Mike and Sam, Ryker already had a list to check on the Internet. And she was sure he was as eager to follow up the leads as she was to import some exotic new flower.

Daria knew she'd built herself a nest where she felt safe to combat her childhood anxiety about forever being shipped off to a new school or summer camp, but she didn't understand Ryker at all. Maybe he'd lived in one Podunk town all his life and had craved adventure.

"Did you move around much as a kid?"

"All the time." So much for her idea. "Remember, my dad was a drunk. He lost his job every few months. We usually moved in the middle of the night, the bill collectors two steps behind.''

''That must have been rough.''

''It was no big deal. Usually exciting.''

''What about being the new kid at school all the time?''

''I was good at sports. Later, most of the kids I knew were online.'' She noted he hadn't used the word *friend.* ''I could plug in anywhere.'' He cast a sideways glance at her. ''Why are we having this conversation?''

''All day I've been thinking that no one I know is turning out to be what I thought. Can we really ever know someone?''

''What do you mean?''

''I've worked with Sam for two years, and I never suspected he would do anything criminal. Or convince Cindy to invest in his scheme. I feel as if everything I've thought to be true is wrong.''

''That's the first sign of a top-notch investigator.''

''Questioning everyone and everybody?'' She felt as though her world had turned inside out, and he was complimenting her because she couldn't make sense of it. ''I don't want to live in that kind of world.''

''The world hasn't changed. You're just looking at it differently.''

''But I don't want to.''

She sounded like a petulant three-year-old, but her life seemed like one surprise after another—all of them bad. Except for knowing Ryker, she wanted to erase the last couple of months. Go back to when—

no matter how distorted—she'd viewed the world through rose-colored glasses.

"Up till now you've led a rather sheltered and pro-tected existence."

"There's nothing wrong with that."

"Except change tends to be uncomfortable when you're unprepared."

She might have trouble understanding him, but he had pegged her with a simple philosophy that she couldn't deny. She and Fallon might not have grown up loved, but they'd never wanted for a thing. And their business had been a success right from the start. While Daria had struggled to achieve her goals, she'd always set attainable goals, easy goals, especially in her personal life.

She'd dated men without letting anyone get close. She'd kept busy with her career, allowing work to substitute for close relationships. She'd never been engaged, or really in love. Never really thought about marriage in a way other than abstract. Because that would require more of herself than she'd been willing to risk. But if she didn't risk her heart, she wasn't ever going to find a soul mate.

Of course, she had to go and have this epiphany now while she was with a man who was unlikely to stay in one place long enough for her to get to know him well. When she could be sent to jail at any time. When she could do absolutely nothing about making some changes.

"Did I insult you?"

She shook her head. "Why would stating the truth insult me? You've given me a lot to think about."

"You needn't worry about being unprepared to handle yourself. I've prepared enough for both of us."

In another man the words might have been a boast. But Ryker had simply stated the facts as he saw them to comfort her. However, something in his intonation told her that she might not like his "preparations."

From that look in his eyes, he was thinking about the case. She wished he would forget work for one more night. Tomorrow was Elizabeth's funeral and she needed to unwind and wondered how much persuasion it would take to get him to make love to her again.

He parked the car in her garage, but instead of getting out he turned to face her. "I've invited a few people to your apartment." He'd invited people into her home? "They're probably already inside."

"But the locks? My alarm?"

"I gave Logan Kincaid the code. And the man's never met a lock he couldn't pick."

"YOU INVITED STRANGERS into my home?" Daria had the urge to slap Ryker's handsome face but she'd probably just hurt her hand. He'd twisted in his seat toward her so they could talk, but Daria didn't want to listen. She practically leaped out of the car and headed toward the parking garage's elevator. Just because she'd allowed Ryker to spend a few nights in her apartment, just because they'd made love and she wanted to do so again, didn't give him the right to let his friends into her apartment without telling her first.

Before she'd taken two steps from the car, Ryker had caught up to her. He grabbed her shoulders, forcing her to turn around. His determined eyes told her that he had no intention of letting her go. But he had no right to stop her.

"What?" she snapped.

"You aren't going up there to insult the people I work with."

"You should have told me you'd invited them into my home." She tried to shove past him.

His voice cracked like a pistol and she might as well have tried to shove a mountain aside. Ryker was rooted like a hundred-year-old oak, his face rock hard. "I made a mistake by not telling you until now."

"Damn right you did."

She tried to twist around him. He shifted directly in her path, blocking her, and she found her back against a concrete post.

He softened his tone. "I guess I'll have to make it up to you."

"Damn right you will."

He might have her pinned so she could neither advance nor retreat, but she refused to back down. His pinning her with his body had her breath coming in gulps and her nostrils flaring.

Ryker lowered his head, placed his mouth over hers and cut off her protest. She had no place to go. He positioned his hands on the concrete on both sides of her head. Trapping her.

She gasped and he took advantage of her open mouth, his tongue slipping between her lips with practiced ease.

And she melted. If this was how he intended to apologize to her, then she'd have to let him make it up to her more often.

He could shut her up with a kiss like this anytime. When he could reduce her to mush, take away her will just by touching his lips to hers, she just wanted to know where this man had been all her life. She lived in the financial capital of the world. And she loved playing Jane to his Tarzan as if they were alone in the jungle instead of right in the middle of a parking garage.

The man sure could kiss, as if he was in complete control, and the sensations darting through her were absolutely yummy. His lips on hers had at first shocked her, then taunted her, then fired her emotions to a new level of intensity. He pulled her close, trapping her hands between them, taking what he wanted, ravishing her mouth.

And she wanted him. Her belly unknotted at the sparks he'd kindled. She didn't want to stop the uncontrollable urge to yield to him utterly and completely. And her heart unlocked like a rosebud in summer sunshine.

At that moment, she was responding to him on pure instinct. Somehow he'd made her wanton. And her body didn't care that her mind was confused at her needy response. She arched into him, her breasts tingling as he crushed her to him. Her heart thundered and her pulse zinged hotter than heat lightning.

He kept his body up close and pressed to hers, but finally released her mouth—after he was good and ready, after he'd proved to her that he could make her head spin anytime he chose.

As apologies went on a scale of one to ten, his had been a twelve. She hadn't expected to enjoy his man-handling. But she liked his chest pressed to hers. She liked that he made her feel wanted.

Thinking clearly while he pressed her against the concrete column was next to impossible. With her thoughts tumbling about, she couldn't say a word, not until she regained her equilibrium. Never in her life had her brain said no while her heart said yes. She needed time to figure out what was happening, why she was reacting with such uncharacteristic passion while they were in the middle of a parking garage where anyone could come by and see them making a spectacle of themselves. Fallon had been the Harring-ton who'd allowed passion to rule her life. Daria was the solid, competent sister, the sensible one. She didn't have flings—only relationships with men who asked before they kissed a woman.

Ryker Stevens didn't ask. He took. He might wear a suit with panache. He might have mastered the in-tricacies of the latest technological advances, but he'd just again proved he had a wild side. And that he hadn't yet released her proved he just might not be done yet, which shot another tingle of excitement down her spine.

He spoke, invading her space, pinning her firmly. "My friends aren't the type to paw through your pant-ies. Logan Kincaid worked for NORAD and NASA, probably programming this country's satellite communications network. His security clearance is classified so high that it's classified.

"Web Garfield is ex-CIA and a master in several different martial arts. If you aimed a gun on him from sixteen feet away, before you could pull the trigger, he could kick the weapon out of your hand.

"Jack Donovan can pilot any aircraft with wings and many without. He's the kind that swoops in to save people while the bad guys are shooting. The man's crazy enough to enjoy risking his life.

"Last but not least is Travis Cantrel. Don't let his laid-back Texas drawl or the diamond twinkling in his ear fool you. He's ex-FBI and the best hostage negotiator in the northern hemisphere."

She listened until he stopped talking. Maybe she'd overreacted. Again. But he should have told her. That was Ryker's fault.

Suddenly she wondered when she'd started blaming him for everything she didn't like. That character trait wasn't attractive.

Be calm.

Think rationally.

But how could she be calm when she could feel his heartbeat right through her clothes? When she could feel his desire pressing into her belly?

Even as she craved the physical sensation of his warmth against hers, his heat inside her, she wished he'd stop crowding her and allow her thoughts to settle down. "All right. I'm willing to take your word that they aren't going to steal my jewelry, but why are they here?"

"They're coming to Elizabeth's funeral tomorrow."

"Why?" And what did that have to do with them staying in her place while she wasn't there?

"Because we need help. I suspect that the killer will be at the funeral tomorrow. I want the crowd on tape. I want certain conversations bugged. And I want you protected. I can't possibly cover all the bases by myself."

"That part sounds reasonable."

"And I invited them into your home because it makes my job easier. I need to brief them. We don't have much time. And I don't want Detective O'Brien catching on to our spying, and interfering with our investigation."

"They're spending the night? I only have the guest room and my office."

"Don't worry, we probably won't get much sleep anyway. And if I need a few winks, I'll double up with you."

"You're presuming a lot."

"Am I?"

"Just because we made love one time—"

He kissed her again, shutting up her protest. And he fired up her senses all over again. No one had ever treated her with such arrogance. But he seemed to know just what she wanted, even before she knew, herself.

She trembled against him in pure female need. His clever mouth knew exactly how to caress hers to stoke a fire that roared to her primitive soul. He was reaching her on an elemental plane, bypassing her brain and heart and searing her right to her feminine core. And despite her feeble thoughts that this was a public place, his domination was utterly delicious.

He pulled back his head and body just enough so she could free her hands. And she had just enough caution left to once again try to shove him away. In a gentle move he captured both wrists in one of his hands and pinned them over her head.

Automatically her back arched, lifting her breasts up to him. She opened her eyes and stared into his face. His eyes gleamed in the semidarkness of the parking garage, revealing enough to see his predatory gleam. And her mouth went dry.

He reached below her skirt and touched the inside of her knee. His feet between hers kept her legs open for him to do as he wished.

He skimmed his fingertips from the inside of her knee up her thigh. His voice was low, husky. "If you don't want me, I'll stop, but I'm not through apologizing."

Her throat was so tight, she couldn't speak. She just stared at him, amazed she could want him so badly that she no longer cared that they were in a parking garage.

His fingers reached the top of her stocking, traced the garter and bare skin, shimmied over bare thigh. All that prevented him from touching her intimately was a tiny scrap of lace. She couldn't stop the quiver in her belly or the trembling of her legs. If he hadn't kept her pressed with her back to the column and pinned her wrists over her head, she might have sunk to the pavement.

"If I touch you, will I find you slick and wet and ready for me?"

"Maybe."

His voice deepened. "You've left me no choice but to see for myself."

In her befuddled state, she thought he would remove her panties. Instead, he lifted her wrists, placed her hands on the one-way sign above her head. She clenched her fingers around the metal to hold herself up.

She should stop him.

But she couldn't bring herself to say one word to end Ryker's delicious onslaught. Not when every cell in her body longed for him to continue.

He stepped back six inches. Just enough for him to unbutton her blouse. "Look at me," he commanded.

He unbuttoned the top button. She swallowed hard, tilted her head back and met the red-hot heat in his eyes with a fire all her own. Slowly he unfastened the second button as her chest rose and fell with impatience. Why was he taking so long with the buttons? Why must he skim his hands over every tiny part of bared flesh before going on to the next button?

Finally, he parted her blouse. Boldly he freed her breasts and the tips hardened with her need to be stroked.

Continuing to hold her gaze, gently he covered each breast with one hand. "Do you know why you're letting me do this?" Her breasts swelled under his caress and she bit her tongue not to beg for more. "Do you know why you want me to continue?"

She couldn't think. Not when he held her halfway

between raw passion and the ultimate pleasure. So she bit her lip and refused to say one word.

When he flicked her nipples with his thumbs, she let out a soft moan. "Someone might come by."

"They might," he conceded with a charming grin.

But probably not. It was the weekend. Almost dark. And she didn't want him to stop what he'd started. Not with her breasts aching and swelling under his masterful touch, not when she had to fight back the whimpers of need in the back of her throat.

Then he dipped his head and nibbled first one breast, then the other, shooting fire to her core. At the same time his hand slipped back under her skirt. He touched her through her panties and she couldn't help thrusting her hips toward him, silently demanding more.

She wanted so badly for him to touch her, stroke the throbbing ache between her legs without the impediment of material. But this was his game and he set the rules.

"Remember in the whirlpool I told you I would take my turn?"

"But—"

"You have any objections?"

"Only that…"

"That what?"

She licked her bottom lip as he teased the admission from her. "You're going too slowly."

"That's because I love the way you respond to me. I love your passion." He moved his finger faster, back and forth over the scrap of lace. "I love you, Daria."

Her head was spinning. Her body was striving for

release and yet, she didn't want to miss a word that he was saying. "What?"

"You heard me. I love you."

And then he dropped to his knees, leaving her breasts bared to the nippy night air. She groaned in frustration as he abandoned her breasts, but when he finally slid her panties down, she had only one thought.

Yes! She wanted him skin to skin.

Suddenly his mouth was on her and she almost screamed with joy, excitement and need. Her breaths came in giant rasps. Her nipples tightened into hard buds. And then with his tongue he urged her higher until she exploded with a muffled shout of excitement.

In that moment, she didn't care where she was or how she'd gotten there. She only knew that never in her life had she blossomed with such intense emotions. She wanted to laugh and cry and dance with the wonder. But she was held fast by Ryker, who would do with her what he wished.

Ryker stood and she wrapped her arms over his head.

Hands on her bottom, he carried her to her car and set her down on the hood. At the cool metal against her bare rear, she grinned. Who would have thought that Daria Harrington could get so carried away that she would have sex on the hood of her car?

She sat up to unsnap his pants. But he was way ahead of her. Already unzipped, he'd produced a condom from his pocket, then slid out of his pants and shorts.

"Hurry."

"Why?" He tore open the packet.

She took his offering and rolled the condom over him in one swift, sure gesture. "Because I want you inside me."

"Why?"

She didn't answer. Couldn't answer. His clever fingers found her again and she leaned back on the hood and wrapped her legs around his waist. He thrust into her, and then held still, except for his fingers that strummed her like a fine guitar.

As the sensations built, quickly, fiercely, she gasped. "Please."

"Please what?"

"Move your hips, damn you."

"Not until you say the magic words."

She would have said anything he asked. Frantic with desire, she lifted her hips to meet him. "I... already...said...please."

"Tell me that you want me."

"Yes."

"Tell me that you need me."

"Yes."

"Tell me you love me."

"Yes."

Every muscle clenched and then released. She screamed his name. He spurted inside her with a lusty groan. And at the same moment, her car's alarm went off in a loud, long siren.

Chapter Twelve

At the sound of the car alarm, Ryker laughed.

Still under him on the car's hood, Daria punched him in the arm. "Get off me."

"Why?" he teased.

She wasn't amused. "The security guard will be here in seconds."

"Okay. Okay. If you insist." He stood, found his pants and removed the car keys from the pocket. After unlocking the front door, he slid behind the wheel, placed the key in the ignition and turned off the siren.

Daria had straightened her bra but had just finished rebuttoning her blouse, crookedly, when the security guard rounded the corner. Still chuckling, Ryker covered his lap with his pants and wondered how long it would take Daria to notice that the guard had spied Ryker's undershorts on the pavement.

"Ma'am? Is everything all right?"

"Fine." Daria finally saw Ryker's navy shorts by the front tire and her lips twitched in amusement. "The alarm went off...by accident. Sorry."

The guard rolled his eyes toward the garage ceiling and strolled away. Daria scooped up Ryker's underwear, walked around the car, opened the door and flopped into the seat, where she burst out laughing.

"I can't believe...that we...that he almost..." She tossed him his undershorts. "How the hell did you talk me into...?"

"Maybe because you love me."

At his words, her laughter subsided. Her smile disappeared. "I never said..."

"Yes, you did. While we were making love. When I told you that you loved me, you distinctly answered in the affirmative."

"I didn't know what I was..." He'd never seen her so flustered, and with her hair messed and her lipstick smudged, he thought she looked adorable. He actually thought about taking her into his arms for a repeat performance in the back seat.

"Lots of people say things they don't really mean when they are in the throes of passion."

At the confusion and dismay on her face, his heart sank like a ship going down in a storm, but he responded by teasing. "Don't tell me that I'm going to have to make love to you again to get you to admit the truth."

"That's not funny." Her mood had changed from happy and lusty and comical to way too dark and serious in the space of a heartbeat.

"I'm not laughing." In fact, if he hadn't possessed an overabundance of self-esteem he might have thought she was using him as a distraction from her problems. But he knew she wouldn't have responded to him so freely unless her emotions were involved. That's why he'd pushed the sexual encounter to the edge, hoping she'd realize that she would never have acted as she had if she didn't love him. His plan had backfired, and now angry at himself, he didn't have a plan B or a preset escape route.

"Why is it so difficult for you to admit that you have feelings for me?"

She hesitated, licked her bottom lip, then finally spoke. "I do…like you."

She liked him. That was like saying he was nice. And he felt nice and insulted. Angry at himself for failing to get her to admit that she had feelings for him, he just barely refrained from slamming a fist into the dash. "So you make love like we just did to every man you merely *like?*"

She removed a brush from her purse and ran it through her hair. "Must we talk about this right now? Your team is waiting in my apartment."

"They can wait."

"I need a shower."

"You're stalling, looking for excuses to avoid thinking about what you feel. If you keep looking hard enough, sooner or later you'll find a reason to push me away for good. Is that what you want?"

He opened the car door, stood and stepped into his shorts and pants. For such an outwardly well-adjusted woman, she certainly had a lot of issues. Sheesh. And she'd had the nerve to tell him that he couldn't make a relationship work. Well, all of his might have been short-term, but at least emotions had been in the mix.

"I'm sorry." Daria came around the car and touched his arm.

He pulled away. Right now he didn't want her touch. Right now he also wanted a shower—to wash away her scent, if only he could as easily wash away the memory of how good it felt to hold her, kiss her, make love to her. He'd never told another woman that he loved her, and she'd thrown his feelings back in his face like rotten garbage.

Okay. Fine. She didn't love him. He closed off the pain. He would deal with her rejection. Later.

First he had a mission to finish—and as far as he was concerned, the sooner the better.

"I said I was sorry," she repeated.

"I heard. You might want to straighten your blouse so my friends don't guess that you've been slumming."

She gasped. "That's not true." She straightened her buttons with shaking fingers.

"Really?"

"Don't think you can take the high ground with me." She fisted her hands on her hips. "Name one thing we have in common."

"Making love in a whirlpool and on the hood of a car."

"Besides sex."

"Now you want to place conditions on my feelings? Well, at least I have them. You're so damn careful to protect yourself that you don't take any risks."

"See. You just proved my point. We're different."

"Damn right."

"Too different to have a future together."

''But not so different that you can't take pleasure when I'm deep inside you, right?''

IT TOOK DARIA the walk from the garage to her apartment to get a grip on the riot of emotions cascading through her like a rushing waterfall. Making love with Ryker had swept her into a current so strong that she'd had no choice but to let him carry her away. Talk about the ultimate rush. She could barely walk in a straight line. Her pulse remained elevated and her thoughts kept tugging her under until she could barely keep her head above water.

And while she struggled to right herself in a world gone topsy-turvy, she'd hurt the one man trying to help her. She hadn't meant to, had only wanted to be honest with him, to let him know exactly where she stood. But now she couldn't seem to keep her feet under her.

Only years of pulling herself together for business meetings no matter what crises she'd just faced moments before let her walk into her apartment with composure.

Ryker strode beside her, his face showing no emotion, his eyes alert. He'd hidden his emotions so easily that if she hadn't known him well, she would have thought they didn't exist. But a telltale clench of the muscles in his jaw and the hard set of his shoulders told her that he wouldn't easily forgive or forget her refusal to love him back.

Ryker only thought he was in love with her. No doubt he equated great lust with a great love, but that wasn't necessarily always so. No doubt he liked her, but he would move on to his next mission and eventually another woman. Time and distance had a way of making feelings fade—even lust.

Daria stepped inside her apartment and a tall, dark-haired man in an immaculate custom suit greeted her with an outstretched hand. "Daria Harrington, I'm Logan Kincaid."

As smooth as his manicured nails, with no rough edges, Ryker's boss gave away nothing. She had no idea what he thought about her. Or if he could tell what she and Ryker had been doing on the hood of her car such a short time ago. While she'd rebuttoned her blouse, tucked it in neatly and brushed her hair, she could do nothing to disguise her swollen lips or ease the electric tension radiating between her and Ryker.

Logan Kincaid's handshake was cordial. She looked him straight in the eye and spoke her mind. "Ryker warned me you'd be here."

"Did he also tell you that we plan to stay until we find what we need?" Logan asked the question as if he already knew that she didn't like friends in her home, never mind strangers. But she sensed an inherent honor in the man that made accepting him easier.

Logan's team had taken over her living area. Computer hardware, communications gear and guns had been neatly placed in the space, and she could see they'd gone out of their way not to disturb her plants.

What surprised her the most was her cat. Ace sat on a crate calmly licking his paws and surveying the scene as if he were king of his domain. And King and Queen were poking their noses out of the plants in curiosity.

Ryker nodded a greeting to the others but spoke to Logan. "You get any intel on Harry's last missions?"

"Web made a few calls."

Ryker introduced the team to Daria, helping her put faces to names, with the information he'd given her earlier. "Web's our contact with the Agency. Jack Donovan's our pilot. And Travis is our negotiator and communications expert."

Web separated himself from his position by the wall and she realized he'd been sitting so still that he drew little attention to himself. When he moved, he had had a certain grace and economy of motion that reminded her of Ace, or a deadly jungle cat.

Web spoke in an understated way that invoked confidence. "I made a few calls. Since Harry's marriage, his missions over the last few years were more diplomatic than dangerous. We don't believe his death was Agency connected."

Daria suspected that Web had a wealth of information that he'd condensed to those few sentences. But she wasn't surprised that neither Ryker nor Logan asked more questions. Apparently they trusted Web's judgment, and information was shared on a need-to-know basis.

The pilot, Jack Donovan, jerked his thumb over his shoulder toward the office where Ryker had set up his equipment. "Your computer's calling you. It's been beeping since we arrived."

"I'm running my pattern-breaker program." Ryker headed toward her office, leaving her alone with his team.

She should have felt ill at ease, but for some reason

she didn't. The men around her were so efficient and professional that she trusted them in her private domain.

"Can I get you men anything? Coffee?"

"No, thank you. If we need anything, we'll fend for ourselves." Logan spoke as team leader but reminded her of a high-caliber business executive. "We'll try not to interfere, but…"

"But?"

"I'm afraid we've already invaded your privacy."

She could tell he didn't mean camping out in her apartment. As if on a signal, Travis, his diamond earring winking, approached. "I listened to your message machine."

Just because she hadn't answered her messages in several days gave him no right. "Did you open my mail, too?"

Logan looked her straight in the eye. "I would if I thought it necessary."

Reminding herself that Logan was trying to help her, she clamped down tight on her emotions. "So tell me, what's on my message machine that's caught your interest?"

"I think you should hear this yourself." Travis retrieved her machine and plugged it into one of the many extension cords crisscrossing the room that now supplied power to all their electronic gear.

"Call me," Mike Brannigan's voice demanded.

The message ended with a beep and moved on to the next one.

"I need to talk to you. It's important."

"That's Elizabeth."

Elizabeth had left her a message! At the sound of her dead friend's voice, at the shock of hearing her speaking as if she were still alive, Daria started to shake. Hearing Elizabeth was spooky.

"That's it?" Disappointment washed through her. She had no idea what Elizabeth had wanted to tell her.

Travis clicked off the machine. Logan led Daria to the bench by the blooming daylilies. He gave her a few moments to think, as if he realized the shock she had received.

Elizabeth had called her the night after Daria had caught her friend with her brother. Daria had been out with Ryker, and when she'd come in she'd been too tired to check her messages. The next day had been too late. Elizabeth had died.

"Are you okay?" Logan asked. "Can I get you a glass of water?"

She shook her head and repeated, "That was Elizabeth."

"Do you have any idea what was so important?"

"She might have been calling to talk to me about my brother. I'd just found out that night that they were seeing one another."

"But?"

"Talking about Peter should have made her happy. And on the tape...she sounded frightened."

"Elizabeth managed your Fifth Avenue store, correct? Could her message have had anything to do with the business?"

"It's possible. But she didn't try to reach me again

the next morning, which she probably would have done if the problem was store related."

"So you think this was personal?"

"I can't be sure but I think so. If only I'd listened to my messages and called her back."

"Could Elizabeth have spoken to her family about—"

"She doesn't have anyone—except, maybe she talked to Peter."

Peter was home from the hospital. He was staying with her folks for a few days so they could keep an eye on him. She knew because she'd called several times today. And not once would Shandra or her father put her call through. Earlier, she hadn't wanted to try his cell phone and disturb him if he was sleeping, but now she didn't hesitate.

Daria dialed her brother and tried to forget how he'd treated her while he'd been in the hospital. "How're you doing?"

"I'm scared to eat anything."

"Peter, you have to eat."

"I know. I know. But if you'd seen poor Elizabeth's face…"

"She left me a message on my answering machine."

Peter's voice rose hysterically. "Oh, God. What did she say?"

"Just that she had to talk to me about something important."

"That's it?"

"Do you have any idea what she wanted to tell me?"

Peter regained control of himself. "I don't know. We weren't at the stage where we shared everything. And tomorrow we have to bury her."

His voice ended on a sob. And she worried about him having a breakdown. He'd lost a sister and a lover, and he didn't sound as if he wanted to talk to her.

He almost died. Of course he's wary.

"Are you well enough to attend the funeral? No one would hold it against you if you didn't—"

"I need to say goodbye."

"But if you aren't—"

"I'm going." He raised his voice defiantly. Yet he seemed fragile. One moment he'd been sobbing, the next angry, as if on an emotional roller coaster.

She didn't want to do anything to upset him. "Okay, Peter. I'll see you tomorrow."

Daria hung up the phone. She realized that Logan Kincaid was an expert interrogator. He knew when to be polite, when to press and when to listen. Right now he let her explain. "Peter doesn't have a clue. He sounds as if he's barely holding himself together."

"And I may know why," Ryker said as he returned from his stint at the computer.

"Maybe because he's lost his sister and his girlfriend and he almost died?" Daria couldn't quite control her sarcasm. Hearing Peter so down and hurting made her feel worse than she already did.

"Harrington Industries is on the verge of collapse," Ryker announced.

"You've probably picked up another rumor," she suggested calmly, considering how worried she was over Peter. Her brother hadn't sounded…stable. But maybe he was overly emotional due to some medications the doctors had given him at the hospital.

"I don't think these are rumors," Ryker disagreed. "You know that money you lent Shandra?"

"Yes?"

"She cashed the check and gave the money to Peter."

"Not my father?"

"The same hour she made the cash withdrawal, Peter made a deposit for exactly the same amount. No wire transfer. The transaction was all cash."

"What did Peter do with the money?" Logan asked.

"He tried to shore up the company, but even a sizable check is just a drop in the bucket. The company is hemorrhaging."

Despite Mike's warnings, Daria still had difficulty believing what Ryker was telling her. Ever since she'd been a little girl, Harrington Industries had been an icon of Wall Street. Solid. Like the Statue of Liberty. Harrington was considered an equal of IBM, General Motors and Microsoft.

"I don't understand."

Ryker paced in front of the bench she shared with Logan. "Peter's in charge of building a gigantic power plant in India."

"So what?"

"He signed a contract with the Indian government to buy electricity from Harrington Industries at whatever price he wanted to sell it."

"Sounds like he signed an excellent contract," Daria commented.

"It looked like it," Ryker admitted. "There were no competing bids."

Logan rubbed his forehead. "I heard rumors that Indian officials are claiming government workers were paid off."

Daria still didn't understand how her father's company could have huge financial problems. As long as the world needed oil and electricity, Harrington Industries should be sound. This wasn't the first time an American company had been accused of bribery overseas, nor would it be the last, especially in countries where nothing got done without a bribe.

"If their tactics aren't ethical," Daria said, "there will be repercussions, maybe the stock will sell off a bit, but the deal still seems profitable. So what's the problem?"

"India just held new elections." Logan sounded as though he was thinking aloud.

Ryker nodded as if to confirm that his boss was on the right track. "The new government refuses to honor the old contract."

"Then the losses will be astronomical," Daria said. "Harrington Industries is capital intensive, and they can't afford to sink all that money into a power plant and then leave it idle. The land alone cost a fortune, never mind the equipment and the huge port they built for the oil tankers."

"Apparently the new Indian government wants to use coal, which is cheap and plentiful, not oil," Ryker added. "People are outraged at what they're calling American industrial imperialism."

Her father probably would have been much happier to have been born a hundred years earlier, when he wouldn't have had to abide by the recent congressional restrictions. However, as far as she knew, Rudolf Harrington didn't break the law. He might bend it to his advantage, but he'd never done anything illegal.

"But even if Harrington Industries is hurting, what does that have to me with me?" Daria asked. But then she knew and she felt as though she'd stepped into a hornet's nest of deceit. "Oh, God."

Ryker stopped pacing, knelt in front of her and took her hand. "I'm sorry."

She pulled her hand back. After their earlier argument, she didn't feel entitled to his comfort. "You think my father poisoned my sister and tried to kill my brother and then framed me so he could take over Harrington Bouquet?"

"And don't forget Fallon's life insurance policy."

"Even five million dollars isn't enough to make a dent in that kind of red ink."

"Unless he wanted to hide your money in some offshore account and declare bankruptcy."

Daria shook her head, unconvinced. "That's not Rudy's style. He loves a good fight."

"Shandra might have concocted the scheme." Ryker was full of nasty possibilities. "Your stepmother's not too fond of you, and although she loves her son, clearly she puts your father first."

Like a cat chasing its tail, Daria's thoughts couldn't

quite catch up with her emotions. She didn't want to think anyone in her own family could be that coldly calculating. "Just because Harrington Industries is having financial difficulties doesn't mean someone in my family is a murderer."

"True. Mike Brannigan is still a suspect." Ryker looked at Logan. "What we need is to bait a trap."

Logan's tone turned thoughtful. "All the players will be at the funeral tomorrow."

"That's why I asked you to come."

Daria looked at Ryker with hope. She needed this to end. She needed answers. Not only did she hate having the possibility of her arrest for murder hanging over her head, she hated having to be suspicious of everyone she knew. The pressure sat on her chest, and she forced several deep breaths.

"You have a plan?" Logan asked Ryker.

Ryker rose to his feet. "More like an idea."

"I'm listening." Logan leaned back. Clearly he trusted Ryker's judgment. They seemed more like partners than boss and employee.

"Suppose we put out the word at the funeral that the police have cleared Daria and are about to arrest another suspect. Detective O'Brien might even be willing to cooperate."

"Then what?" Daria asked.

Ryker paced. "We watch and we listen."

"That's it?" She couldn't help her reaction.

But Logan nodded his approval. He stood. "I'll take the men and prepare the site."

Ten minutes later, Daria sat with a cup of tea at

her kitchen table across from Ryker. "What exactly does watch and listen mean?"

"We tap every phone. We bug the grounds so we can hear every conversation. And we watch each move every suspect makes. If we're lucky, someone may panic or slip up."

"And if they don't?"

"Then we'll be here in your apartment for at least another day."

Chapter Thirteen

Daria spent the night pacing. Sleep was out of the realm of possibility. Between her worries over the next day and her argument with Ryker, she couldn't rest. Every time she closed her eyes she saw the pain on Ryker's face when she'd claimed that she didn't love him.

She'd only been telling him the truth. She stared out her bedroom window at the city below and barely noticed the traffic fighting through the gloomy rain-soaked streets or the people hurrying under umbrellas. Her concentration focused inward. His questions tormented her. Especially the one about their lovemaking. Why *had* she enjoyed their sexual encounters so much? Why had she allowed him to push her into a possibly compromising position is such a public place?

She had never done anything like that before. And if her previous partners had suggested such antics, she would have refused. But she hadn't refused Ryker. She found herself caught up in the excitement, enthralled by the thrill.

As the hours of the long night slowly passed, Daria

found no answers. She kept hoping Ryker wouldn't come to her room, and yet, when he didn't, she kept looking at the closed door in disappointment.

She'd allowed herself to depend on him for support. Now she no longer had that luxury. Even though he would stand at her side at Elizabeth's funeral, she no longer felt entitled to lean on him or share her grief and pain.

A cold and gritty rain fell in light showers through the night, and by morning dark clouds blocked the sun and the rain fell like tears from heaven, a perfect match to her black mood.

After dressing in a charcoal-gray skirt and blouse, Daria joined Ryker in the kitchen. She'd expected the rest of the Shey Group to still be here to act as a buffer, but she and Ryker were alone.

He sat at her kitchen table wearing khaki slacks and a short-sleeved black shirt. He'd hung his suit jacket over the back of his chair and seemed unconcerned that Ace had settled in his lap and might leave cat hair behind.

Ace curled into a ball, tucked his head on his paws and purred happily, the traitor. Her cat hadn't even visited Daria last night, apparently preferring his company to hers.

Ignoring the awkward and simmering tension that existed between them since yesterday, Daria made herself a cup of comforting tea.

She peered down the empty hallway but didn't see any other members of the team. "Where's everyone?"

"At the cemetery. It takes time to set up listening

devices that will cover every sound from a sneeze to a whisper.''

"When did they leave?'' she asked and then, after she saw the knowing look in Ryker's eyes, wished she could take back the question. It was one thing to believe he hadn't joined her in order to stay with his friends, but quite another to know that he'd been alone...and that he hadn't come to her.

"It's been just us since 2:00 a.m.'' His eyes gleamed with speculation. "Didn't you sleep well?''

"I didn't sleep at all.''

He raised one arrogant eyebrow, then leaned back in his chair, stroked the cat and challenged her. "Why not?''

It was none of his damn business why not. She wasn't about to admit that he was a good part of the reason for her sleepless night even if he already suspected it.

She checked her watch. "Shouldn't we be going?''

He totally ignored her question, asking one of his own instead. "Were you hoping I'd come to you?''

Daria let out an exasperated sigh. "What difference does it make?''

"Do you usually want a man so soon again after you've made love?''

She didn't like his personal questions. Didn't like how he kept pushing her to examine her own emotions. And she certainly didn't have to stand there in her kitchen and put up with his silky insinuations that her feelings ran deeper than she wanted to admit. Leaving her tea behind and plucking the car keys from her purse, she strode toward the front door. She could drive herself to Elizabeth's funeral. In peace.

He could catch a cab or jog through the rain, she didn't care which, as long as he wasn't with her.

As if reading her mind, he rose to his feet. "We have to arrive together. To the rest of the world, we're still…a couple."

She gnashed her molars so hard she was surprised she didn't crack a tooth. That he was right just made her angrier.

She slung her bag onto her shoulder. "Then let's go. I don't want to be late."

"You don't want to talk to me?" he teased.

"That, too."

"Maybe we should only make love. You enjoyed my company then. I especially liked those tiny noises coming out of the back of your throat—"

She glared at him. "Will you just shut up?"

"And let you give me the silent treatment? I don't think so."

She grabbed her umbrella from the stand in the foyer. "Did anyone ever tell you that you are the most aggravating man?"

Ryker locked the front door. "Women usually find me easygoing."

"They must not know you well."

"And you do?"

She had no intention of answering any more of his questions, or responding to his provocative comments. She didn't want to think about him. She was going to a good friend's funeral and she didn't want him to…distract her.

She cast a sideways glance at him in the elevator. He never looked innocent. How could he with those knowing eyes? But was he deliberately trying to make her angry so her grief wouldn't cut as deep?

He knew which buttons to press to irritate her. But was he handling her so smoothly that she almost hadn't noticed?

She changed the subject back to the investigation. "Am I expected to do anything special?"

"Stay next to me at all times. Speak normally but try to pick up on any unusual behavior."

"Like what?"

"Inappropriate talk. Anyone who goes out of their way to avoid you or someone who wouldn't normally say hello who does."

"The bugs will pick up all the conversations simultaneously?"

"Travis will monitor communications from a van. Jack Donovan will be flying overhead in a chopper if he can get clearance to take off in this rain."

"And Web and Logan?"

"Web plans to stick close to Brannigan. Logan will circle."

"Mike might notice."

"Web's a pro. Trust me. Mike won't notice him, and if you do bump into Logan or Web, try not to make eye contact or even nod. I'd prefer you didn't indicate that you know anyone in the Shey Group."

"Okay."

"There's one more thing." From his tone, she knew whatever he was about to say was serious. He reached into his pocket and extracted a small gun. "For you."

"I don't want it."

"Look, here's the safety." He showed her a tiny switch. "This is locked and now the gun won't fire. Turn the switch up and all you have to do is point and pull the trigger."

She stared at the weapon but didn't take it. "Why would I need a gun with the entire Shey Group around me?"

"You probably won't need it." He opened her purse, slipped the gun inside then snapped it shut. "But I feel better knowing you have it."

They reached the parking garage with the gun weighing down her purse. She didn't want to think about carrying a weapon. She couldn't shoot anybody.

She also couldn't keep back the memories of making love against the concrete pole. And the hood of her car. She must have been insane. Or crazy in love. She'd have to think about it later.

DARIA AND RYKER arrived at the New Jersey cemetery in a little less than an hour. The rain had slowed to a drizzle, but Daria still needed her umbrella and opened it as she exited the car. Ryker clasped her elbow and led her to one of the tents where a crowd of mourners milled about and spoke in somber tones.

When Tanya spied Daria and hurried toward her, surprise and gratitude made Daria halt in the soggy grass. Tanya even wore a dress and pumps. Daria had never expected to see her here, and if she'd known she'd planned to attend, Daria would have offered her a ride.

Tanya hugged Daria. "I wanted to be here for you. I know you and Elizabeth were tight."

"Thanks." She embraced the girl and held the umbrella over both of them. "How did you get here?"

"Took the subway to the train station and then caught a cab." Tanya might have attention deficit hyperactivity disorder, but she could navigate the city and surrounding areas like a pro.

Daria's eyes teared at Tanya's thoughtfulness. Many others here would not be so kind.

"The flowers you sent are awesome. Especially the spray on the casket."

"The pansy orchids, did they arrive?" Daria asked. The striking blossoms with deep pink buds had been Elizabeth's favorite.

"Yeah, along with sweetheart roses, calla lilies and the purple freesias. The daffodil wreath is too much. You really outdid yourself."

"Shh. Most people don't know that I—"

"And you don't want them to know because…?" Ryker asked.

"It doesn't matter."

She didn't want people to think she'd paid for the burial and service and had donated the flowers out of guilt. She'd done so out of love. It was the least she could do for her good friend.

Daria heard whispers and snippets of gossip as the three of them approached the chairs. She hoped the hidden microphones picked up every word. Maybe someone would make a mistake. Once under the tent, she collapsed her umbrella.

Several people turned their backs and walked away. Tanya squeezed her hand and then slipped to the edge of the crowd.

Daria searched for her family. Instead, she bumped into Mike Brannigan. Ryker immediately steadied her, and somehow he ended up between her and Mike. Daria didn't believe Ryker's movement was accidental or a coincidence.

Mike wore a tailored dark brown suit and black tie in an expensive-looking silk. His eyes speared her with concern. "You holding up okay?"

She nodded. "Thanks for asking."

"There's a rumor going around that Detective O'Brien is about to arrest a suspect."

"Anyone I know?" She raised her chin and squared her shoulders.

Ryker's plan to plant a rumor had succeeded. Everybody was wondering who would be arrested.

Knowing the plan and carrying it out was more difficult than she had expected. Especially when she wanted to sit in a chair, lose herself in the fragrance of the flowers and remember good times with her friend.

When she spied Isabelle sitting with Cindy and Sam, her first instinct was to mutter an excuse to leave Brannigan and Ryker and join her employees for the minister's service. But her stepmother and father approached, halting her forward progress across the indoor-outdoor carpeting.

Her father looked as if he'd aged ten years since

the last time she'd seen him. The soured India deal must be straining his company even more than she'd thought.

Dark circles and wrinkles under his eyes attested to too many late-night meetings and a lack of sleep. "Daria."

"Hi, Dad." She hugged him for appearance's sake. In public, he always wanted the family to appear closer than they were in private.

Her stepmother looked overdressed with pounds of gold jewelry weighing her down, but she was immaculate as always. With her hair and makeup professionally done and in a designer black dress, she could have posed for *Vogue*.

"Shandra." The two women pretended to kiss one another's cheeks, but smooched air in order not to mess their makeup. A mannerism Daria hated, but now was not the time to draw more attention to herself by shunning Shandra.

Her stepmother whispered in her ear, her tone gloating and loud enough for those nearby to hear. "I heard the rumors, but I still think *you* did it."

"You do?" Ryker pressed.

"Oh, yes. She'll get just what she deserves." Shandra glared at the exotic flowers as if the sight of them offended her.

"This is no time for a squabble," her father muttered. "Sheathe your claws, Shandra."

Just then organ music floated through the speakers, and people took their seats. Ryker led Daria up the center aisle. Heads turned to watch them pass by, but she didn't acknowledge the stares.

Her eyes focused on the white lacquer casket that held Elizabeth's body. Not too long ago, Harry and Fallon had lain like this, side by side, in another cemetery. No amount of beautiful flowers could ease the heaviness that squeezed her heart.

The minister spoke, but she didn't listen. Instead, she remembered happier times, midnight chocolate fests, cramming for exams, convincing Elizabeth to manage the Fifth Avenue store. Their college years had been busy, the years after even busier. Sometimes they hadn't talked for days, but then they'd get together and it was as if no time had passed since their last visit.

Goodbye, my good friend. I will miss you.

The minister had asked if Daria wanted to say the eulogy, but she'd refused, and now she was glad that she had.

If only she'd checked her message machine that night and returned Elizabeth's phone call. What had her friend wanted to tell her? Daria supposed that the mystery might haunt her for the rest of her life.

When the minister finished speaking, Ryker handed her a handkerchief. Daria wiped the tears from her cheeks. She hated the next part of the funeral the most, but she would do this last act for Elizabeth and stood with the other pallbearers to roll the casket toward the mausoleum. Peter walked directly behind her, her brother's face too white, too tight and full of pain.

Coming to the funeral so soon after he'd been released from the hospital might be too much for him. A light sweat had broken out on his forehead, his eyes were glassy, and she wondered if he could be feverish. After they placed the rain-spotted casket in Elizabeth's final resting spot, Peter stumbled into Daria.

"Peter?"

"Not now. Don't say a word," he ordered softly. He wrapped his large black raincoat around her.

Something pointed and hard jabbed her ribs. She tried to move away from the hard pressure, but Peter grabbed the front of the raincoat, trapping her against his side and keeping her there with the pressure from a weapon in his other hand. To everyone else, they would appear as brother and sister, helping one another through a trying time, with Peter trying to protect her from the rain.

But her brother had a gun at her side.

Daria should have been scared, shocked, surprised. But all she could think was that poor Peter had gone crazy with the loss of Elizabeth and blamed her.

She didn't dare say a word.

"I'm taking you to the car." Peter nudged her with the gun and she stumbled, but he held her upright.

Ryker couldn't possibly know anything was wrong, but he fell into step beside them on her other side. She didn't dare glance at him or say a word. Peter had obviously lost his mind. He could start shooting at random.

And suddenly her fear spiked. Not just for herself but for the other people around them. If he fired in this crowd, there was no telling who would go down.

"You okay?" Ryker asked.

She nodded.

"She isn't fine," Peter disagreed, his voice soft and

syrupy with fake concern. "Look at her face, she's as white as Elizabeth's casket."

"We're parked over there." Ryker pointed.

Panic washed her thoughts in a wave of terror. She had to warn Ryker or the Shey Group. None of them knew anything was wrong. Or did they? Peter's behavior was odd, but odd enough for anyone to take notice? And the bugs at the ceremony would pick up his words, but they were ambiguous.

Her brother's eyes were red-rimmed from tears, glassy and hard with his grief and fury. Obviously overcome by his distress at the loss of Elizabeth, his actions might seem perfectly natural considering the circumstances. With Ryker walking beside them clueless, he clearly intended to accompany her in her car.

She didn't want him there in danger of catching a stray bullet. If she said something, would Peter shoot her?

However, opening her mouth to speak would put her life on the line. But she would risk it to ensure Ryker's safety. And that's when the thought struck her like lightning. She loved Ryker. And eventually she would have to do something about it. But not now.

With her heart skating into her throat, she took a chance. "Ryker, my brother and I need some private time together." Peter dug the gun harder into her side, warning her to speak with care. But at least he didn't shoot. "Why don't you take Peter's car back into the city?"

While keeping the gun in her side, Peter dug into

his pocket and then handed Ryker his keys. "Thanks. I'm four cars back. The navy Cadillac."

RYKER DIDN'T LIKE leaving Daria, but with the bug he'd fastened onto her purse when he'd slipped the gun inside, he'd be able to not just track her but eavesdrop on her entire conversation with her brother. Peter had seemed ready to crack under his grief, so Ryker had agreed to her request.

Ryker found the Cadillac without any trouble and pulled out right behind Daria, who was driving. In the heavy downpour, Ryker couldn't see inside the other car that well, even with his efficient windshield wipers. But through his earpiece he listened to the crystal-clear conversation in the other car.

"Peter," Daria spoke softly. "Surely you don't believe that I would poison my best friend."

Peter cackled, his laughter out of control. "You have no idea what's going on in my mind."

"Well, I'm not psychic. Why don't you tell me."

"Take the Holland Tunnel."

"Sure."

Now, why would Peter make such a bizarre request? They'd driven here through the tunnel and would naturally go back the same way without him giving directions. Was he cracking up, or simply stating the obvious?

Peter's voice broke on a sob. "You must have heard the rumors about the India deal falling apart."

"You couldn't have known the new government wouldn't uphold the contract."

"Dad blames me." Peter said. "His entire company is at risk. I've got too many responsibilities, too much on my plate, too much riding on me. You don't know what the pressure is like with everyone depending on me. I've got to fix things.''

''Of course you will.''

Peter started to shout. ''Don't hand me platitudes.''

At the undertone of violence and despair in Peter's tone, Ryker, suddenly uneasy, closed the distance between the two cars. He adjusted his frequency. ''Jack, you up in the chopper?''

''Not in this weather. You have a problem?''

''I'm not sure. Why don't you drive toward the city, just in case I need backup.''

''I'm ten minutes out.''

''Thanks.''

Ryker tuned back to Daria and Peter's conversation. Although the radio remained clear, the rain beat down so hard that he had to turn up the volume to hear over the pelting drops.

Peter sounded as if he was sobbing. Could he be having a nervous breakdown?

''The money Mom gave me is just a fraction of what I owed. So I went to Sam for a loan.''

''You went to him instead of a bank to keep the problems private,'' Daria guessed.

''With his outrageous rates, I owe him hundreds of thousands in interest alone, and he's sending some goons after me.''

So, Daria's college bookkeeper, Sam, did have connections to organized crime. He used his job with Daria as a cover. Of course Sam had lied. He'd told them that to make collections he used the phone, but

Peter knew how criminals dealt with unpaid loans. No wonder he was afraid.

"Why didn't you ask me for help?"

Peter's tone turned sly. "You don't have that kind of cash, but you will after you collect Fallon's insurance money." The bad feeling in Ryker's gut started to knot. "And when I collect on the policy—"

Daria gasped. "What are you talking about?"

Had Peter just threatened Daria's life? Ryker wasn't sure. Both Fallon and Daria had huge life insurance policies made out to one another. Peter couldn't collect unless both women died, and they'd named him next in their wills.

"For a smart woman, you don't have a clue. You think your little brother is cracking up over the loss of his dear Elizabeth. But she betrayed me."

"Because she knew you owed Sam money? Was that what she wanted to tell me?"

Peter let out an odd-sounding sigh. "Elizabeth didn't know about the business. She felt bad about letting me into your apartment to use your computer. She suspected that I planted the e-mails, stole the backup tapes and wiped your drive, and she wanted to tell you, but I stopped her."

"It was you! Oh, God." Daria must have understood the implications just as Ryker did.

"All of you betrayed me," Peter whimpered. "Fallon wouldn't give me the money I needed, but now she will, and so will you."

Ryker pressed the gas pedal to the floor. He spoke to the team. "You recording this?"

"Got it," Travis acknowledged. "I think Peter's about to make a move on Daria."

Ryker hadn't seen this coming. He'd suspected Mike Brannigan and her father, maybe Shandra. But Peter? The beloved, grieving little brother?

And now Daria was sitting in the car, trapped with the bastard.

Although she had to be terrified, Daria sounded calm. "Of course I'll give you whatever money you need."

Peter cackled again. "You still don't get it, do you? I killed Harry and Fallon and framed you so I could inherit your business and the life insurance."

"You wouldn't have inherited until I died."

"Murder is easy to arrange in jail."

Oh, God. Peter had killed Fallon and Elizabeth and Harry. Daria started putting the pieces together. "And you swallowed that poison on purpose to throw us all off?"

Clever. The sick bastard's ploy had worked. Once he'd been poisoned, they never considered him a real suspect.

Ryker prayed that Daria would remember the gun. That she'd have the guts to turn it on Peter to protect herself.

Damn! Damn!

Daria had known her brother was dangerous when she'd found an excuse to send Ryker to the other car. She'd known something was wrong. But how? Peter hadn't said anything suspicious or the hidden mikes would have picked it up and he'd have heard. Ryker recalled the raincoat. Any number of weapons could have been hidden beneath it.

Daria hadn't been white-faced due to the funeral. She'd been terrified. But she'd tried to protect him— at a risk to her own life. And Ryker hadn't even suspected her ruse.

"I only ingested a little of the poison, and I vomited immediately. I had no idea it could make me that sick."

"I'm so sorry."

"You're going to be more sorry," Peter crowed. "Once we go through the toll, I'll duck down, and you'll appear to be driving alone. The cameras will give me an alibi when I claim to have gotten out of the car."

"Why do you need an alibi?"

"Because you're going to write a note, admitting your guilt before you kill yourself."

HE INTENDED TO kill her. Daria had to keep Peter talking while she stalled for time, but her stomach sickened, especially when she knew his plan might work. She needed to think, to do something drastic. Crashing the car at high speed would only kill both of them. And she couldn't retrieve the gun from her purse, hide her action from Peter and drive at the same time.

Think.

She'd have to slow down at the tollbooth. Could she open the door and run before Peter grabbed or shot her? When she slowed down for the toll, perhaps she should smash her car into one of those concrete pilings.

What else could she do? Trying to talk him out of killing her didn't seem likely, not after he'd admitted to murdering three people.

Her silence had him stroking the gun. She had to distract him.

"How did you know that you were in our wills?"

"Your lawyer's secretary thought she was in love with me."

"And causing the computer to disappear from the police evidence room?"

He shrugged. "I had nothing to do with that. I intended for them to find your e-mails. Some cop's kid is probably playing Half Life on your computer as we speak."

The tollbooth came into view, and she swung smoothly into the far left lane, praying he wouldn't suspect, fighting to keep her face calm, her breathing even. She slowed, opened her purse. Peter would think she was reaching for her wallet. Her fingers closed around the gun.

Peter kept his weapon pointed at her, but beneath his raincoat so the toll attendant couldn't see it. Daria took a slow deep breath, braced, then jerked the car to the right, slamming toward a concrete barrier.

At the same time, Ryker's car careened out of nowhere, the blue Cadillac blocking her car from exiting the toll. Metal crunched, specifically the front right fender caved. She'd missed her target.

She'd been aiming to strike the passenger door to pin Peter inside.

Her air bag popped open, slapping her face, making breathing difficult.

A gunshot fired. She expected pain, a burning sensation. But instead she could again breathe. Peter's shot had missed, hitting and deflating the air bag.

She had to run before he fired again. Pinned by his air bag for several critical seconds, he wouldn't take long to recover.

Daria fumbled to release her seat belt, shoved open the door and, gun in hand, ran toward Ryker, who crouched on the hood, his weapon aimed at the air bag and Peter.

"Get down," he ordered.

A second shot fired from inside the car. She screamed, fearing for Ryker's safety. And then she was in his arms.

For several long moments she stood within the circle of his embrace just appreciating the comfort he could give. Her heart battered her ribs and her blood roared in her ears, blocking out the commotion around her. Daria didn't move as police sirens closed in on the scene. She wanted to stay right here with Ryker, letting him comfort her.

"I never thought...I had no idea...I was so scared..." She tried to turn her head toward her brother.

But Ryker placed his back between them. "Don't look. He killed himself."

As Detective O'Brien approached, Daria realized that she still had no proof to clear her name. This might be the last time she could hug Ryker without handcuffs on her wrists. Because with Peter gone, she was left to take the blame.

"Are you all right, Ms. Harrington?"

"She's just shaken."

"Travis patched through the recordings to my squad car. If you can get me a copy of the tape, I can close this investigation."

She raised her head to look at Ryker. "Tape?"

"I slipped a bug onto your purse. From our tech van, Travis recorded everything Peter said during your conversation."

"You bugged me?" Mixed emotions simmered through her, surprise and shock, then gratitude and elation mixed with a bittersweet tenderness. "You could have told me."

"You weren't in a listening mood."

She pulled back from Ryker just enough to face O'Brien. "You aren't going to arrest me?"

"You're free to go. Maybe tomorrow you could come down to the station to give a statement?"

"Okay. Sure. Yes." She was free, free to live the rest of her life, thanks to Ryker and the Shey Group.

Gently, Ryker took the gun from her numbed fingers. "You won't be needing this anymore."

"I won't?"

"Not with me here to protect you."

"But—"

"I know you love me." And she did love him. She hadn't chosen to fall in love. Love had just happened. He might not have roots in the city, he might leave her to go on missions, but she loved him.

"You risked your life trying to keep me out of danger," he said.

"You knew?"

"Not then. I figured it out as I listened to your conversation. But I know now, and I'm not letting you walk away."

"So much has happened, I'm not sure…"

"I'm willing to wait until you are."

"But suppose—"

In typical Ryker fashion, he didn't let her speak. His mouth came down over hers. For once she had no hesitation, no doubts. He might not be what she'd thought she wanted. But she'd been wrong. This man was meant to be hers.

Epilogue

One year later

Daria squeezed Ryker's hand so hard he winced, but he didn't think of complaining. Not even when his lovely wife cursed at him.

"You son of a bitch, I'm never letting you touch me again."

"Okay."

She panted. "You could at least argue. Help me keep…my mind off the pain."

In the childbirth classes they'd taken together he'd learned that women in the transition stage were often irrational, that they said things they didn't mean. He let her insults slide off his shoulders like rainwater. Right now she could swear a blue streak and he wouldn't care what she said. The joy she'd given him this past year, the happiness they'd found together as husband and wife, was worth any harsh words she'd tossed his way.

And now she was giving him children. His heart swelled with love. Marriage had been good for both of them. For the first time in his life he had a real home.

And so did she.

He already felt attached to their children. He'd talked to them every night while they were in her womb, getting them accustomed to his voice as he massaged Daria's swelling belly with oil to try to prevent stretch marks. Not that he cared about a few little marks, but Daria had insisted.

He only wished he could take her pain for himself. The pregnancy hadn't been easy. She'd carried the twins to full term and had spent the last month in bed. She had made a kind of peace with her father and stepmother. While she would never be close to them, she'd tried to include them in her life.

Her forehead broke into a sweat and she glared at him. "You did this to me."

"I did," he acknowledged, showing no outward pity. He needed to be strong for her, but his stomach felt as though he'd just hit zero g in one of Jack's chopper maneuvers. Was having children supposed to take this long? Cause so much pain? For twenty-four hours she'd labored, but the doctor had insisted she was doing fine.

With a cool cloth, Ryker wiped the sweat from her forehead. "Perhaps you should let the doctor give you the epidural."

"No."

Stubbornly beautiful and opinionated as always, she panted through the next contractions. She didn't want drugs, preferring to let nature take its course.

"Ryker, you owe me."

"Whatever you want," he agreed. He would agree

to anything for her ordeal to end, for her to finally rest.

Finally the doctor gave her permission. "On the next contraction push."

Ryker slid behind Daria's shoulders until she rested against him in a half sitting, half reclining position. "You can do this. Almost there."

He murmured encouragement in her ear, talking, coaxing, pleading and telling her that she was so brave. So strong. He had no idea what he said.

"The head's crowning. Push," the doctor ordered.

She scowled at everyone. "I...am...pushing."

She sat up a little more, bore down with a grunt of determination. Ryker could feel her body tensing, her muscles contracting.

"The baby's coming. I've got the head. The shoulders. It's a girl. She looks good."

Daria flopped back into his lap. But she had only seconds to rest.

Ryker's attention focused on Daria. "One more time. You're almost done."

Within the next sixty seconds she gave him a son. Two babies. Two perfect babies, one at seven pounds two ounces, the other at seven pounds even.

While the medical people did their work, he held Daria in his arms, stroking her, massaging her tense shoulders. When a nurse handed each of them a baby, his heart overflowed with happiness at the dual blessing.

He kissed Daria. "Thank you."

"Oh, my. Aren't they precious?"

He grinned. "I counted all the fingers and toes. Twenty of each. Two perfect sets."

''I'd like to name them Fallon and Harry. Would that be all right with you?''

Mind naming his son after the man who'd saved his life? No, he wouldn't mind at all. ''I'd like that.''

Tiny Fallon opened her eyes and waved a fist in the air. Her brother yawned, then sucked on his forefinger.

Daria, her eyes bright with joy, the pain seemingly over and behind her, smiled at their babies, then at him. ''You've given me so much. I thought making a home was the most important thing, but home is living with you. I love you.''

The words that had once been so difficult for her to say came more easily to her lips now. And Ryker couldn't have been more pleased that he was the one she'd married, that he was the one she'd chosen to father her babies. Winning her trust hadn't been easy and he vowed never to let her go.

He kissed each baby on the cheek.

''Hey, where's my kiss?'' Daria demanded with a contented smile.

He leaned over and kissed her on the mouth. ''I love you, too. Very much.''

* * * * *

For a sneak peek at the next book in Susan Kearney's HEROES, INC. *series,* SAVING THE GIRL NEXT DOOR, *to be published in June 2003, turn the page....*

Prologue

The cop wouldn't be sticking her nose where it didn't belong, not anymore, not after some intensely smooth computer hacking. Thanks to a back door in the police department's computer program and two ''solid citizens'' who'd come forward and accused her of taking a bribe, detective Piper Payne had had her chain yanked good and tight.

She'd better get used to being out of the loop. Hung out to dry.

But just in case she persisted in her annoying inquiry, she now had bugs on her phone, worms on her computer and a miniature tracking device in her wallet.

She would be watched.

And if she made another wrong move, the chain would tighten around her neck. She wouldn't just lose her job, she'd lose her life.

Chapter One

Jack Donovan had a reputation for attaining success—even if it required dive-bombing his chopper through a hailstorm of bullets, but if he'd known what waited for him down below, he might never have landed.

When he was a Navy SEAL Jack had scuba dived five oceans and climbed mountains on four continents, nevertheless, with his instinctive timing and superb reflexes, he'd been born to fly. For the military he'd flown test aircraft, and for his current employer, the Shey Group, he flew everything from gliders to jets to helicopters.

Blissfully unaware of his fate, Jack couldn't have ordered a better day for flying the chopper. The Florida sky above the Gulf of Mexico shimmered a rich silky blue that was full of promise. With not even a hint of a thundercloud in sight, Jack cruised above Clearwater's sandy shoreline with no more on his mind than his anticipation of landing smoothly, then kicking back with an icy brew in a honky-tonk bar along the beach where he could watch the sun set over the gulf.

He sighted his landing field. At one thousand feet above his target, Jack powered down his engines. Man and machine plummeted toward the earth. If he had been in a plane, he'd have had to dive the nose down to pick up enough speed to glide. But in a chopper, he maneuvered his hands and feet to autorotate the rotors, a basic landing maneuver that every pilot practiced in case the engines conked out during a flight.

Without his heart even skipping a beat, Jack lightly touched down and abandoned one dream vehicle for another, his latest acquisition, a Mercedes coupé. He chose his cars like his women—fast and sleek and ready to run. After striding across the tarmac to his silver convertible, which had sat all afternoon in the baking sun, he slid behind the wheel. The leather seat was hot enough to make him wince.

He'd forgotten how extreme a Florida summer could be. Although Jack had grown up in Clearwater, he hadn't been back home in years.

Bad memories of fights with his parents during his wild and reckless teenage years had kept him away. A decade ago Clearwater hadn't been a big enough town for Jack Donovan. Except for spring break when college students flocked to the community's tacky souvenir shops and powder-sand beaches, the sleepy beachside town wasn't a happening place.

Jack turned on the radio and air conditioner full blast. As Black Sabbath blared from the speakers, he pressed a button that caused the Mercedes's hardtop to automatically fold into the trunk.

Yes, baby. Wind and sun and surf, here I come.

Years ago, Jack had yearned for Paris, Tahiti and Nepal, and the navy had given him the means to fulfill his dreams. He'd since circumnavigated the world by boat and plane more times than he could count. The navy had also given him the discipline to turn him into a productive citizen.

Now he worked for the Shey Group, a private team of men, formerly with the military or one of the intelligence agencies, who charged high fees to take on missions that required special skills and classified connections. The Shey Group allowed him the luxury of this silver coupé with its souped-up engine that could go from zero to sixty in 4.6 seconds. Not to mention his friends, the elite of the elite. Good guys to have at his side in a brawl. Not that Jack anticipated a fight. Not while on vacation.

Whistling, contented, he burned rubber, exiting the private airport. The car handled like the high-priced luxury item that she was, and he headed for the beach.

A cute yellow VW Bug pulled out behind him.

At the next corner, Jack turned right. So did the yellow VW.

He might be on vacation, but Jack's normal observant skills kicked in. That's why he could take so many chances and still have all his body parts—he took *calculated* risks. Just for the hell of it, he made two right turns and then another left.

The VW Bug stuck to him like a flea.

Dark-tinted windows prevented him from identifying the driver. But Jack no longer had any doubt someone was following him. He had several choices. Since the VW could never match his speed, he could accelerate and lose the tail. Or he could confront his pursuer and find out what in Sam Hill was going on.

Intel first. With a grin of pleasure, Jack pressed his foot down on the accelerator.

The car matched his speed. The other driver was determined. Careful.

He sped through a green light and headed for the highway. The VW stayed right with him.

Impressive. The driver of the other car didn't come too close, and yet Jack couldn't shake him, not without a flat-out race on the interstate. Exciting perhaps, and a choice he might have made as little as five years ago, but no matter how much he wanted to stomp the pedal to the metal, he couldn't justify the risk to civilians.

However, now that he had some idea he was dealing with a professional, he thought back over his last few missions. All of them had been sewed up tight. Logan Kincaid, his boss, didn't leave loose ends. But perhaps one of the team was working a case that he hadn't been brought up to speed on yet.

Jack turned down the heavy metal blaring from the radio and hit the call button of his cell phone.

"The Shey Group," an evenly modulated secretary's voice answered.

"Logan Kincaid, please."

"Bored with your vacation, Jack?" Logan's warmly modulated voice came over the speaker phone.

His boss might not be in his office, but he was usually available. Using state-of-the-art technology, Logan had his calls forwarded to his cell phone so he could be reached 24/7, pretty much anywhere in the world. "Ready to take on your next assignment?"

"Sheesh. I just got here."

"So you aren't calling because you missed us, yet. What's up?"

"I called to ask you the same question."

"I don't understand."

"Any operations working that I should know about?"

"We're practically shut down."

"Then there's no reason for someone to be tailing me?"

"Damn it, Jack. You haven't been down there twenty-four hours and you already have some jealous—"

"I haven't even checked into a hotel." *Yet.* "I spent last night with my folks." A tense, awkward evening he'd prefer to forget. How could they have raised a child and then have nothing to say to him except criticism? In short order, they'd disparaged his career. His friends. His lack of a family. His wheels. And his haircut. You'd have thought he had come home with five earrings and a tattoo, instead of this sweet little coupé.

"Don't your folks turn in around eleven?"

Logan never forgot a detail. He'd once overheard Jack calling his mother to wish her a happy birthday. She hadn't been pleased when Jack had roused her out of a sound sleep at 10:30 p.m. And Logan knew that Jack was a night owl and hadn't gone to sleep before midnight since he'd started shaving. So no doubt Logan thought he'd been out partying and had

taken someone else's honey home and the car following was a jealous lover—but it wasn't like that.

"You need any help?" Logan offered.

If Jack asked, his boss would mobilize a team
within twenty minutes. Jack lived for that kind of loy-
alty, something his parents wouldn't ever comprehend.

"I can handle it."

"You sure?"

"Yeah. I hardly think a yellow VW Bug would be
the choice of an assassin."

He rechecked the side mirror. The car was still following him.

"Fine. Try not to get any speeding tickets."

Jack chuckled and let his foot ease off the gas. Just
because he had superior reflexes and could handle
high-speed maneuvers didn't mean the local cops
would appreciate his breaking the law.

For the moment he adhered to the speed limit and
allowed the tail to come after him. During his stint in
the military Jack had learned the value of planning.
He would pick the time and place for the confronta-
tion with his mysterious pursuer. Someplace private.
Where there was no chance of innocents catching a
stray bullet.

Jack leaned over and opened the glove compart-
ment. Driving with one hand, keeping his attention on
the road, he reached for his gun. He tucked the
weapon into the front of his jeans and checked the
rearview mirror.

Soon. He would make his move.

Jack veered from the highway to the off ramp. Two

miles farther, he turned into an industrial section of town. He passed several rough-looking bars and crossed a parking lot to a dilapidated warehouse that squatted beside a chain-link fence overgrown with chin-high weeds. If he remembered correctly, the doors of the warehouse had long since been scrapped, leaving him a dark, private spot in which to corner his pursuer.

Jack drove around the back of the warehouse and stepped on the gas, heading straight for the doorless entrance. He entered the building, jammed on the brakes and hauled on the wheel, whipping the car around until he faced the entrance.

Within seconds, he'd exited his vehicle and taken cover in the shadows by the opening. He flicked off the gun's safety and aimed. Timing was critical.

The VW slowed, then halted just outside in the sunlight.

Come to me.

Just a little more.

The driver flicked on the headlights, and Jack averted his eyes to avoid being momentarily blinded. The car edged forward.

While the sight of his car distracted the driver, Jack lunged toward the Bug and the driver's door. He yanked on the handle. Employing several smooth moves, he pressed the gun to the driver's temple, locked his free arm around her throat and dragged her from the car.

A woman. Too surprised to resist?

Her hair was auburn, the fragrance scented by sunshine. Jack had yet to see her face, but bad people also came in curvy shapes and one-hundred-and-ten-pound packages. With her back pressed to his chest, he couldn't mistake the hard bulge of her harness and gun poking his ribs.

The female was armed.

"Don't move one freakin' finger. Don't so much as breathe hard, sugar."

Odd. She still hadn't tensed. Didn't fight him.

Instead, she chuckled. "Oh, Jack. You always were such a hothead. You going to pat me down?"

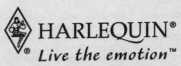